TEMPT ME, YOUR GRACE

YOUR GRACE

LEAGUE OF UNWEDDABLE GENTLEMEN, BOOK 1

TAMARA

COPYRIGHT

For all the horse-loving people in the world. You'll forever be my tribe. And for my Arabian beauty, Don Don. You gave me endless hours of love and fun and I'll never forget how fast you could go, or how much you loved to run.

PROLOGUE

Knight Stables, Berkshire, 1816

Miss Avelina Knight, Ava to those close to her, tightened the girth of her mount, and checked that the saddle wouldn't slip whilst hoisting herself onto one stirrup. With a single candle burning in the sconce on the stables' wall, she worked as quickly and as noiselessly as she could in the hopes that the stable hands that slept in the lofts above wouldn't wake.

Pleased that the saddle would hold, and that her mount was well watered before her departure, she walked Manny out of the stables as silently as possible, cringing when the horse's shod feet made a clip clop sound with each step.

Ava blew out the candle as she walked past it, and picking up her small bag, threw it over her horse's neck before hoisting herself up into the saddle. She sat there a minute, listening for any noise, or the possibility that someone was watching. Happy that everything remained quiet, she nudged her mount and started for the eastern gate.

There was still time and she didn't need to rush, now that she was on her way. Tate had said he'd meet her at their favorite tree at three in the morning, and it was only half past two.

She pushed Manny into a canter, winding her way through several horse yards that surrounded her home and past the gallop her father used to train their racing stock. Or what was once her home. From tonight onward, her life would finally begin. With Tate, she would travel the world, make love under the stars if they so wished, and not have to be slaves to either of their families' whims or Society and its strictures.

Tate and she would find a new life. A new beginning. Just the two of them until they expanded their family to add children in a few years.

Pleasure warmed her heart at the knowledge, and she couldn't stop the soft laugh of delight which escaped her.

In time, Ava hoped her father would forgive her, and maybe when they returned, happily married with children even, her father would be pleased.

The shadowy figure of a man stood beneath the tree. Yet from the stance and girth of the gentleman, it did not look like Tate. Coldness swept over her skin, and she narrowed her eyes, trying to make out who was waiting for her. Her stomach in knots, she pushed her horse forward unsure what this new development meant.

Ava looked about, but could see no one else. With a couple of more steps she gasped when she finally made out the ghostly form. Her father.

Her heart pounded a frantic beat. How was it he was here and not Tate? They had been so careful, so discreet. Why, they had not even circulated within the same social sphere to be heard whispering or planning. With Tate being the heir to his father, the Duke of Whitstone and Ava only the daughter of a racehorse notable, their lives couldn't be more different.

Ava rode her horse up to the tree. She saw little point in turning back.

Pulling up before her father, she met his gaze, as much of it as she could make out under the moonlit night.

"Ava, climb down, I wish to speak to you."

His tone was not angry, but guarded, and the pit of her stomach lurched at the notion that something dreadful had happened to Tate. Had he been hurt? Why wasn't he here to meet her instead?

She jumped down, walking up to him, her mount following on her heels.

"Papa, what are you doing here?" she asked, needing to know and knowing there was little point in ignoring the fact that he'd found her out.

She dropped her horse's reins, and her mount reached down to nibble on the grass.

Her father's face took on a stern cast. "The Marquess of Cleremore will not be meeting you here, Ava. I received a note late last night notifying me that, as we speak, his lordship has been sent to London to catch the first boat out to New York. From what his father, the Duke of Whitstone, states, this was the marquess' decision. Tate confided in his father the predicament he'd found himself in with you, and that he didn't know how to untangle himself from having to marry a woman who was not his equal."

Ava stared at her father, unable to fathom what he was saying. Hollowness opened up in her chest and she clasped her shawl as if to halt its progress. Tate had left her? No, it couldn't be true. "But that doesn't make any sense, Papa. Tate loves me. He said so himself at this very spot." Surely she couldn't have been wrong about his affections. People did not declare such emotions unless they were true. She certainly had not.

She loved Tate. Ava thought back to all the times he'd taken liberties with her, kissing her, touching her, spending copious amounts of time with her and it had all been meaningless to him. She had been a mere distraction, a plaything for a man of his stature.

Her stomach roiled at the idea and she stumbled to the tree, clutching it for support. "No. I do not believe it. Tate wouldn't do that to me. He loves me as I love him and we're going to marry each other." Ava stared down at the ground for a moment, her mind reeling before she rounded on her father. "I need to see him. He needs to tell me this to my face."

"Lord Cleremore has already left for town. And by morning, he'll be on a ship to America." Her father sighed, coming over to her and taking her hand. "I thought your attachment to him was a passing folly. His lordship was never for you, my dear. We train and breed racehorses and, in England, people like us do not marry future dukes."

Ava stared at her father, not believing this was happening. She'd thought tonight would be the start of forever, but it was now the beginning of the end. Her eyes smarted and she was powerless to hold onto her composure. "But I love him," she whispered, her voice cracking.

Her father, a proud but humble man from even humbler beginnings, straightened his spine. "I know you think you did, but it wasn't love. You're young, too young to be throwing your life away on a boy who would have his way with you and then marry another titled, well-connected woman."

"I'm not ruined or touched, father. Please don't speak

in such a way." She didn't want to imagine that Tate could treat her with so little respect, but what her father said was worth thinking over. The past few weeks with Tate had left very little room other than to plan, to plot. Would they have thought differently, would Tate have acted differently if he'd been older, more mature? If his departure showed anything, it was certainly that what her father was saying was true. He had regretted his choice and had left instead of facing her. Letting her down as a gentleman should, had not been his course. It showed how little he thought of her and the love she'd so ardently declared to him.

She swiped at her cheeks, wanting to scream into the night at the unfairness of it all.

"I'm sorry," she said, looking at her half boots and not able to meet his gaze. *How could he have done this to me?* She would never forgive him.

He sighed. "There is one more thing, my dear."

More! What else could there possibly be to say! "What, papa?" she asked, dread formed like a knot in her stomach at her father's ashen countenance. She'd seen a similar look from him when he'd come to tell her of her mother's passing and it was a visage she'd never wanted to see again. Ava clutched the tree harder.

"I'm sending you away to finishing school in France. I've enrolled you at Madame. Dufour's Refining School for Girls. It's located in southern France. It comes highly recommended and will help prepare you for what's to come in your life; namely, running Knight Stables, taking over from me when the time comes."

Finishing school! "You're sending me to France! But Papa, I don't need finishing school. You know that I'm more than capable of taking over the running of the stables already. And I know my manners, how to act in both upper- and lower-class society. Please do not send me away. I won't survive without you and our horses. Don't take that away from me, too." *Not when I've already lost the happiness of which I was so certain.*

He shushed her, pulling her into his arms. Ava shoved him away, pacing before him.

Her father held out his hand, trying to pacify her. "You'll thank me one day. Trust me when I tell you, this is a good thing for you, and I'll not be moved on my decision. We're leaving for Dover tomorrow and I, myself, will accompany you to ensure your safe arrival."

"What." She stopped pacing. "Father, please don't do this. I promise not to do such a silly, foolish thing again. You said yourself Tate was leaving. There is no reason to send me away as well." Just saying such a thing aloud hurt and Ava clutched her stomach. To have loved and lost Tate would be hard enough; nevertheless being sent away to a foreign country, alone and without any friends or support was too much to bear.

He came over to her, pulling her against him and kissing her hair. "This is a good opportunity for you, Ava. I have worked hard, saved, and invested to enable me to give you all that a titled child could receive. I want this for you. Lord Cleremore may not think that you're suitable for him, but we shall prove him wrong. Make me proud, use the education to better yourself, and come home. Promise me you will do so."

Ava slumped against him. Her father had never been flexible on things and once he'd made a decision it was final. There was no choice; she would have to do as he said. "I will go as I see there is little I can say to change your mind."

"That's my girl." He pulled back and whistled for her mount.

She couldn't even manage a half-smile as Manny trotted over to them.

"Let us go. I'm sure by the time we arrive back home breakfast will not be far away."

Using a nearby log, Ava hoisted herself up onto the saddle. The horse, as if knowing her way home, started ambling down the hill. Light shone in the eastern sky and glancing to her left, Ava watched the sun rise over her land. Observed the dawn of a new day, marking a new future even for her, one that did not include Tate, Marquess Cleremore and future Duke of Whitstone.

A lone tear slid down her cheek and she promised herself, there and then, never to cry over Tate again or any other man. She'd given him her heart and trust and he had callously broken them. That the tear drying on her cheek would be the last she ever afforded him.

And his precious dukedom that he loved so dearly. More dearly than her.

CHAPTER 1

*S*o many miles separate us. I do not sleep with the thought of you. When did your love for me perish? I cannot fathom why you would not confide in me that your feelings had changed, maybe even moved on elsewhere…

— An excerpt from a letter from Miss Ava Knight to the Duke of Whitstone

Knight Stables, Berkshire, 1821

Ava pushed her newly purchased mare, a fine sixteen hands thoroughbred that had breeding to rival her own, into a blistering gallop. She smiled, sitting low over the neck of this precious girl, and they started around the corner and down the home straight of their family gallop.

Her stable manager and trainer, Mr. Greg Brown, stood watching from the side of the gallop, hearing his exuberant shouts as she went past him in blistering speed.

She smiled, impressed with her horse's unfathomable swiftness.

The early morning mist started to burn off the grass and trees, freshness in the air after a light shower of rain. Pulling up the mare, Ava kept her in a slow trot to return to Greg. The mare blew steam out of her nostrils with each breath and Ava patted her, giving her a congratulatory rub.

Ava breathed deep herself, marveling at the beauty of her life, the beauty of this place that was now hers.

"What did you think, Greg? Do you think she has a chance at Ascot?" Ava teased, knowing they had a lot ahead of them before they could even think to enter the mare into such a race there.

He chuckled, bending under the railing and coming out to pat the horse himself. "Maybe next year if she keeps performing as she is. She'll have to prove herself at Epsom before then, though."

Ava kicked her feet free of the stirrups and jumped down. She handed the reins to Greg and walked around the horse, checking to make sure she was sound after her run. "Gallant Girl will prove herself, just as her name suggests, you wait and see. And with the new yearlings in a year or so that we'll produce with Titan breeding with Black Lace, we'll have more beauties like this one."

"About Titan," Greg said, pulling off his cap and running his hand through his hair. "There may be some difficulty having him cover with Black Lace as you wanted. I got word today that Mr. Tuttle has sold him."

Ava paused in her inspection of the horse and placed Gallant Girl's front right hoof down. She met Greg's gaze and read that he'd not been making a joke. "Titan's been sold? But Mr. Tuttle promised my father that if we gave them the first foal off Black Lace two years ago, that he would allow us to have Titan to cover Black Lace this year. My father held up his end of the bargain, and you're telling me that he has not?"

She started for the stables, yelling out to one of the young lads to saddle up Manny. Greg followed her as fast as he could while leading Gallant Girl beside him. "Wait, Miss Ava. Wait. I do believe there are options other than Titan that you should consider."

There was no other horse better than Titan and if Mr. Tuttle thought to swindle her and her late father, why, she would take back that little foal, Beatrice, and be damned the scandal in the racing world. How dare the man cheat them in such a way? He'd shaken her father's hand, damn it. Didn't that mean that the agreement was as waterproof as a ship's hull?

"There is no other horse as fine. I want Titan to sire the next generation of foals here at Knight Stables and there is nothing anyone can say to change my mind. You know as well as anyone that he's the best thoroughbred in England, possibly on the continent as well. His height, along with his strong blood lines and speed, makes him the only horse that'll do."

Ava thanked the lad who saddled up Manny for her and, clutching the saddle, she hoisted herself up.

"Where are you going?" Greg asked her, clutching the reins under her horse's neck.

She frowned at his impertinence. He let go. "I'm going to find out what Mr. Tuttle is about treating my stables with so little respect. I may be a woman, and my father may be gone, but we had a deal. I'll not stand for it."

She turned her mount and kicked Manny into a canter, heading directly for Tuttle Farm. When her father had been alive, nothing of this sort of underhanded business ever took place. They would never have thought to cheat her dearly departed papa. But here she was, a woman, and being treated with so little respect.

Anger simmered in her blood, and even by the time she trotted into Tuttle Farm's yard, her temper had not waned. She spotted Mr. Tuttle lunging a horse in the lunging yard and walked her mount up to the fence, waiting for him to notice her.

His look of contrition told her he knew exactly why she'd come.

"How could you, Mr. Tuttle? You had an agreement with my father that still stands with me," she demanded, forgoing all pleasantries.

The older gentleman yelled out for a nearby stable lad to take the rope and whip and walked over to the fence. He seemed to have aged in the last few months since she'd seen him. As she looked down at his gray, receding hairline and whiskers to match, a little of her temper eased.

"I had no choice, Miss Ava. In fact, if you do not purchase your foal back from me, you'll be buying her back at auction."

She frowned. "What is wrong, Mr. Tuttle? Has something happened to force you to sell Titan and Beatrice?"

He sighed, his shoulders slumping at the words. "It has, my dear. I don't mind telling you as our families have known each other for many years, but I made a bad investment last year and, well, it'll cost me the farm. We're preparing to move to Bath where my wife, Rose, has family. Selling Titan, at least, enabled me to pay off the most pressing debt. With the sale of the house, the land, together with the horses of course, we may have a little left over to keep us for a few years in reasonably comfortable conditions." He met her gaze, his eyes glassy with unshed tears. "I'm sorry, Ava. I know how much you wanted Titan's bloodline."

Forgetting about the horse, she said, "Can I help at all? Is there anything that I can do to ease the debt and enable you to stay? These stables have been in your family for three generations. I would hate to see you lose it all."

"Well," he said, looking about his property, the love he had for his land evident in his gray orbs. "When one makes a mistake, one must own it. I'm just sorry that my wife and my children will lose all that we've worked so hard to build. And I thank you, Miss Ava, but I cannot accept your generous offer. It wouldn't be right."

She nodded, wanting to press, but Mr. Tuttle had always been a proud man. To force him into anything had never worked before and she could not see it changing now. And she did not want to part having argued with him, even if she wanted so very much to help. "Very well, but do let me know if I can support you in any way. Or if there is something you do not want to be sold off to anyone else that maybe I can purchase. At least you'll know who has it and that it'll be loved."

"You're a good girl. And know that I would never have reneged on our deal if I could help it. There really was no other way around it."

Ava adjusted her seat, watching the horse that was being lunged who seemed quite interested in their conversation instead of doing what it was supposed to be doing. "May I ask whom you sold Titan to? Maybe I can negotiate with them."

He looked down at his feet, shuffling them a little.

"Mr. Tuttle," she ventured when he didn't reply.

"As to that, my dear. Well, that is to say…"

What was wrong with the man? "Mr. Tuttle, tell me. Surely, it is not a secret."

He met her gaze and, for a moment, she wondered if he had been sworn to secrecy. Surely not?

"The Duke of Whitstone purchased Titan, Miss Ava. I heard from your father, you see, all about your family falling out with them and, well, I'm sorry that for you to have Titan cover your mare you'll have to go through his grace."

Her hands shook at the mention of him and she clasped the reins tight, anger simmering in her veins at having heard his name. Even after all these years. "Why did you sell it to him? I could've matched the price you wanted."

He shook his head, again shuffling his feet like a naughty school child. "He came here only yesterday and offered cash. I've had money lenders down my back for weeks, so I took it without thinking. I'm sorry, Ava. But I had to think of my family."

Damn it! "I understand," she said, unable to hide the disappointment in her tone. The Duke of Whitstone could be a persuasive gentleman from what she understood. The stories she'd heard about Tate in London did not resemble the boy she'd once loved. If anything, he now sounded like a man who only sought pleasure and cared for little. In the year since she'd been back in England, he'd not once called to apologize for his treatment of her all those years ago.

Ava turned her horse, preparing to leave. "Do come by before you leave, Mr. Tuttle. Bring your family and we shall have tea and cakes. I am disappointed about the horse, but I'm more disappointed you've been placed in this situation. I wish it were not so."

He tipped his hat, bowing a little. "You're very generous, Miss Ava, and we shall call around to say our farewells."

"Very good." Ava waved and started toward home. She kicked her mount into a gallop and swore. Damn the duke and his interfering ways. If only she'd heard of Mr. Tuttle's struggles earlier, she might have been able to help him, or purchase the horse instead of the duke doing so. In her estimation, the duke was not worthy of such high standard of horse.

She could not face having to deal with him either for that matter. That he had not called was a blessing, for she certainly had not wanted to see him and his ugly, lying heart.

But it did not solve how she would gain access to Titan for her breeding program. It was a dilemma she hadn't thought she'd have to cross. But the stallion was paramount to supplementing her bloodlines, possibly siring future winners, and enabling the farm to prosper and never have to face the same fate that Mr. Tuttle has had to.

To give up on her dream to become the best and most esteemed breeding and racing stable in England wouldn't do. She'd given up previously on things she'd wanted, marriage and a family with a man she'd thought loved her, but she wouldn't in this regard. The duke would not take this away from her as well. She would send her manager, Greg, over to the ducal property and have him negotiate if at all possible.

And with any good fortune, the whole breeding program could be accomplished without his grace or her having to step one foot near each other. Just as she preferred.

*T*ate Wells, the Duke of Whitstone, leaned back in his leather-bound chair behind his desk and steepled his fingers as he listened to the Knight Stables' manager lay out the suggested terms for allowing Miss Ava Knight access to his prized runner, Titan.

Not that he would tell the old man, who was as loyal to Ava as her own father had been prior to his death, that hell would have to freeze over before he'd allow her anywhere near his property or Titan. It had been five years since he'd seen or thought of the woman, and he wasn't about to start now.

He shifted on his chair, his mind mocking him for the lie that was. Hell, he thought of her often. Hoped she was well and happy. Even when he went down to the local inn and had a tankard of ale, his ears would always prick up with the mention of Knight Stables and the mistress who ran the successful horseracing farm.

Even so, he would never forgive her for having him sent away. His being in America had stopped him from saying goodbye to his father. By the time news of his father's illness, two years ago now, had arrived in America his departure for England had already been too late. He'd arrived in Berkshire two weeks after his father had been placed in the family mausoleum.

Another hurt he could lay at Ava's door. Or Miss Knight, whose soul was as black as a moonless night.

"Therefore, you see, Your Grace, it would be beneficial if we were to have Titan cover our mare, Black Lace. Miss Knight is willing to pay handsomely for the service and I, along with your own head trainer, can organize all the particulars regarding the horses so you and Miss Knight need not be disturbed."

Tate met the older gentleman's gray gaze, his eyes a little watery with age. So, Ava didn't wish to see him, did she? Well, there at least was one part of the agreement on which they could concur. A small part of his heart ached at the notion that she wanted nothing to do with him. Her severing of their relationship, of leaving England had been so different from the girl he'd once known. There was a time when they could not be kept apart, when every hour, every minute was spent together.

Tate shook the unhelpful thought aside. "I'm not interested in breeding Titan at present. We're looking to have him race in Ascot next year, which I need not remind you is less than eight months away. I do not need the horse taxing himself if it's not necessary."

"I beg your pardon, Your Grace, but horses run and tax themselves daily. To breed the horse will be no more vigorous than training."

Which was true, not that Tate was going to abide by those rules. And he liked the idea of Ava not getting what she wanted. She had ripped his hopes for his future from beneath him. Marrying the woman he loved, respected and adored, not simply a woman who was considered suitable to become a duchess. "It is too much for my horse and I'll not allow it. Please tell Miss Knight to look for another stallion elsewhere for her breeding program."

The older gentleman wrung his cap in his hands. If this deal was so very important to Ava, why hadn't she come and asked him herself? He'd taken great pains in not running into her here in Berkshire and, so far, he'd been successful in his plan.

To know that she was back from France, had been for a year, it was nigh on improbable that they'd not run into each other thus far, even at race meetings and such. Tate thought on it a moment and wondered if she, too, was avoiding him as much as he avoided her.

He stood. "I'm sorry to have wasted your time, Mr. Brown, but my decision on this is final. Please let Miss Knight know." He held out his hand. "Good day to you, sir," he said, ending the conversation.

Mr. Brown stood his shoulders slumped. Tate felt for the man. He would now have to go back and face Ava. It was certainly not something even Tate would enjoy. At least, when he'd known her well all those years ago, she had been determined as much as opinionated. Two traits he'd once adored about her. They had been friends before he'd fallen head over boots in love with her. She had never backed down on a subject if she thought he was incorrect with his thinking, going to great pains to make him see the sense in her judgement. Her determination, her fierce brown eyes alight with fire when she spoke of making Knight's stables the best known in England and with Tate by her side. Ava had always expected the best of people. What a shame she was not able to live up to her own standard.

Mr. Brown shook his hand. "Thank you for your time, Your Grace. Good day to you."

Tate watched him leave. He sat back in his chair, leaning back, thinking on who Miss Knight was today. That she'd not come here and asked herself for the use of Titan was telling, indeed. It seemed all their association of years past meant very little to her. *That they were truly strangers.*

Not that such a realization surprised Tate. The day she'd sent a missive telling him she would not marry him had been enough to tell him exactly what Miss Knight thought of him. Of how much she'd lied and teased his boyish ideals.

Tate ran a hand over his jaw. Even with all that had passed between them, all the hurts, he couldn't help but wonder if she still looked the same. Did she still have long locks that were as rich as chocolate? Were her eyes as brown and wide? Were her cheekbones as high, or had they filled out a little with age?

The clock chimed the hour and, picking up his quill, he pulled the estate paperwork before him and started to check the finance ledgers for the stables and his tenant farms. What did it matter how much she'd changed? He'd changed, too, moved on.

The past two years as duke, he'd been lax in attending to the running of his estates, but no more. It was time he ensured the people who lived off his lands were well cared for. That his racing stable here in Berkshire grew and prospered as he'd always wanted. To make his stables better than the Knights' three miles from here was a good enough motivation to be here instead of town. And with Titan in his stables, he already had the upper hand in moving his plans forward.

Tate pushed thoughts of Ava from his mind, just as she'd thrown him away without a backward glance. No one who was so disloyal and self-centered deserved a minute of his time. Not ever again.

CHAPTER 2

*A*va pushed her horse into a gallop, the roofline of Cleremore Hall, named when the family only had the marquessate emerged from the trees. In only a few moments, she would see Tate again. Be once more in the hallowed halls of the Duke of Whitstone's home. It had been years since she'd ridden this close to his estate, and nerves pooled in her stomach at the thought of seeing him again.

Had he changed as much as she? Five years was a long time, and he'd been away in America for three of them. She supposed that could change someone very much, make them more *worldly*, knowledgeable even. Over the years, she'd secretly listened to the idle gossip about the great family whenever she heard it, wanting to hear if Tate had married or was engaged. Nothing of the kind had ever been mentioned but, upon his return to England, his antics in London certainly had been all that was on anyone's lips. In this county at least.

The man was a veritable rogue from all accounts and, somehow, the notion that he had many lovers, or at least took women to his bed on a regular basis, left the hollow-ness of his betrayal open like a gaping wound.

It was also not who she'd thought he was. Tate had certainly never been such a man when she had known him but they'd been a lot younger then, only nineteen in fact. His grace had also refused to marry her. So, she supposed, maybe if he had been legitimately attracted to her and loved her, he would've taken her to his bed as well. He had not.

She pulled Manny up on a small incline not far from the ducal horseracing stables, and from here she could see Titan eating grass in an adjacent paddock. Clicking her tongue, she pushed her mount forward in the direction of the stables, wanting to speak to the head trainer. See if she could get him to barter with the duke, who seemed to be a stubborn oaf, all of a sudden.

She tied up her mount to a nearby railing, leaving her with enough rein to nibble the grass. The stables were as large as hers, and yet the wood did look in need of fresh paint. At least hers were in better condition, much better than a duke's.

Entering the stables, she stood inside the darkened space and gave her eyes time to adjust. Men went about their business, some boys shoveling out days' old straw from the stalls while a couple of younger lads sat oiling the stirrups on the leather saddles.

"No oats today. He's getting fat," a familiar voice said and she gasped at hearing Tate again after all these years. The thought of fleeing entered her mind for a moment, before she raised her chin and faced the inevitable reunion that was bound to happen now that they were both back in England.

He walked out of a stall and she took the opportunity

to drink in his form, his features, while he was unaware of her presence. The youth she'd once loved was no more. His soft brown hair looked sun kissed, longer on top than the sides and he'd pushed it back without thought giving it a ruffled appearance. His straight nose and chiseled jaw were as perfect as ever and, even now, she recalled the feel of it. Tate's lips were pulled into a half smile after talking to his workers, and she marveled at the fact that one man could be blessed so generously with good looks.

Certainly he was a good four inches taller, and as for his arms that once had been spindly, the current Duke of Whitstone's were muscular and strong. His thighs, encased in tan breeches, bulged with lean muscle and heat bloomed on her cheeks. She bit the inside of her cheek. Even after all that had passed between them, that her body betrayed her by longing for one more caress, a look, a kiss...

What a silly little commoner she was.

He turned and started when he spotted her. A flash of pleasure crossed his features before he blinked and it was gone, replaced with annoyance.

"I will not change my mind, Miss Knight. You're wasting my time and your own."

She sighed, lifting her chin. "I had an agreement with Mr. Tuttle before you forced him to sell you Titan. I deserve for that agreement to be upheld."

He turned, giving her his back. If he meant it to be a slight, he was sadly mistaken. Instead of infuriating her, her body simply had a mind of its own and her gaze dipped to his bottom. Biting her lip, she fought not to grin at how perfect he still was down there.

"By and by, Miss Knight, should you be dressed in such a way? You look like a man."

She raised one brow, still staring at his bottom since he

was still looking the other way. "Like I care what you think, Your Grace. I didn't come here to discuss our clothing, but horse stock. What will it take for you to give me Titan so I can have him cover my mare, Black Lace? I'm willing to pay if its money you want. I remember well how much your family adores currency."

He did turn at that and she narrowed her eyes. Good. She wanted him annoyed. Annoyed as she was, that it was because of her lack of connections, of titled ancestors in her bloodline that had made her so ineligible for him. He'd left for America, abandoned her instead of telling her to her face that he'd made a mistake. That he no longer loved her and didn't wish them to marry.

She would've been hurt, to be sure. But that hurt would've healed knowing that he'd been honest and had acted the gentleman. The man before her was a coward who ran away instead of facing his responsibilities. He'd left her alone and vulnerable. Her school friends had been her salvation, but upon returning to England there was no one. With her father gone, she'd been alone, without protection and she'd paid for that lapse in the worst way possible. She would never forgive him for that.

"You would not have enough funds even if I were to ask that of you."

His words irked and she came to stand not a foot away from him. "I have plenty of blunt, duke. And I'm sure had your father still been alive, I could've bought Titan ten times over by now. So tell me, since the apple never falls far from the tree, what is your price? What will it take for me to have Titan?"

His attention moved over her face and her stomach fluttered at his inspection. What was he thinking? Did he think her much changed since he'd seen her last? Up close, Ava could see the slight shadowing of stubble on his jaw. His clothing, instead of buckskin breeches and superfine coats cut to perfection to fit his form, were tan breeches, knee-high boots, shirt and brown coat. No cravat or waistcoat, no highly starched shirt or polished boots. Ava glanced down at his chest where the tie had come loose on his shirt and the sprinkling of chest hair could be seen. Her fingers itched to feel it again. Once, when they'd been alone, they'd kissed with such passion that she had touched his person, and he too her.

The memory of it made her ache and she ground her teeth, hating that her body would deceive her with the enemy before her.

"He's not for sale," he said, staring down at her, his hardened words brooking no argument.

She narrowed her eyes. "Still stubborn I see, Your Grace." She turned about and started for the door, the click of his boots following quickly behind her. "America didn't cure you of that trait," she threw at him.

He clasped her arm and spun her to face him. She gasped, slapping his hand off of her as his touch left her burning for more. For five years, she'd not reacted to a touch as she'd reacted to Tate's and the hunger in his eyes told her he damned well knew what his presence did to her.

"What do you know of me or how I am? Do not throw insults, Miss Knight, simply because you've not got your way. I could say myself that your stubborn streak has not been trained out of you either. I would've hoped the French finishing school would've been more thorough in your education."

Ava fisted her hands at her sides. "Oh, do not worry, Your Grace. My education taught me a great deal. The most important of all was what type of gentleman to stay away from, vile lechers such as yourself." It had not taught her so very well though, and she pushed that ugly memory away, not wanting to relive that horror that had nothing to do with the man she was currently arguing with. Ava strode over to her horse and hoisted herself up. "Which I intend to do right now."

"Lecher?" he said, his eyes wide. He caught the reins of her horse and stopped her parting. "You know as well as anyone I was never a lecher."

She raised her brow mockingly. "Really, so the gossip in London about you is wrong? You're not a rake? A man who has too many lovers to count? A man who prefers folly to looking after his many estates? Tell me, duke, did the women of New York not satisfy you enough that you had to return home and sow your wild oats here? How very changeable you are from the young man I once knew." Ava shut her mouth with a snap. How had the conversation about Titan escalated into an slaying match between them? All of which was too personal, and too telling. She didn't want him to know that he'd hurt her all those years ago. Had broken her heart.

"I beg your pardon, Miss Knight, but I fail to see why you should care. Do not lob your insults at my head when you're no angel."

"What?" she said, aghast. "What do you mean by that?"

He glared at her. "And now you play me a fool. Good day to you, Madam." He stepped back, giving her leave to go. Throwing him one last glance, she kicked her mount into a canter and left. The ride home was a blur, her blood pumped loudly in her ears over a conversation about a horse that had turned into a fight about their relationship and broken engagement.

Not to mention her lack of manners in bringing up the fact that he'd slept with half of London. The rumors that his estates lacked attention, of which she had no solid proof, was true. She cringed. What was wrong with her?

Ava took a calming breath and nudged her horse into a gallop. She would not allow his boorishness to rile her. He wasn't worth it, and yet, the hurt that had been etched on his face when she left just now had opened an old wound she'd thought long healed.

～

*T*ate ran a hand over his jaw as the delectable bottom of Ava's galloped off up his drive. What woman rode about Berkshire in men's breeches? It would seem Ava did so and with little care as to who saw her or what they thought.

The moment that she'd walked into his stables, his heart had jumped in his chest at seeing her again. He'd had to physically stop himself from taking her in his arms and telling her how much he'd missed her. Within a split second of the thought, the memory as to why they'd not married had reminded him why he would need to be wary of the woman before him. She'd pushed away his love for a chance to travel abroad and study. To run away from being a duchess as it was so very distasteful to her, or so her letter had said.

But, blast it, she was as pretty as he remembered her. Her long dark locks tied loosely at the back of her head, a delicate red ribbon the only article holding it in place. Her eyes were as fierce as ever, burning with passion, or loathing in his case, but still seeing her again had quenched his thirst after being thirsty for so long. He frowned when he lost sight of her, wanting her to come back and give him another set down if only to see her perfect little nose rise high in the air.

"Was that Miss Ava Knight?" his closest friend, Lord Arthur Duncannon said, looking up the drive and in the direction Ava had disappeared. His lifelong friend never missed anything he thought might be fodder for gossip. If it looked juicy and worth commenting on, he always had an opinion.

"Yes," Tate said, starting back toward the house. He didn't want to discuss Ava any more than he wanted to discuss why his heart wouldn't stop pounding in his chest. Or why her words cut him like a sword. She seemed angry at him, considering she'd pushed him aside for foreign shores.

Duncannon caught up to him. "The very one who jilted you? The same Ava Knight who runs the horseracing stables next door?"

Tate glared at his friend and hoped Duncannon would get the hint that this conversation and Ava were not up for discussion.

"Tell me, Your Grace. Or I shall have to find out another way."

"You will not," he said, his voice brooking no argument. "All that you need to know is that we're neighbors and certainly not friends. The past was nothing but a foolish childhood infatuation that is well over on my behalf. And from my conversation with Ava just now, so too it would seem is hers."

Duncannon threw him a disbelieving look, even so much as to scoff a little at his words. Tate halted. "What now, man? What is it that you're concocting in that minuscule mind?"

His friend grinned. "From watching you two from the stables, I would suggest that the feelings that are so very over between you two are not. In fact, I would lay good blunt down and say that, if anything, you both still care for each other more than you're willing to admit."

Tate fisted his hands at his sides. "I do not care for Miss Knight and you need to keep your opinions to yourself lest you're shuffled off to London to live with your mother."

Duncannon held up his hands in defeat. "Very well, I shall not say another word. But do tell me, what did she want to discuss? It seemed she wasn't very happy when she left."

Unhappy was calling what Ava was feeling lightly. She was mad as hell if he knew her at all. At one time, there hadn't been another person in the world who knew her as well as he did. In the past, after a disagreement such as the one they just had, Ava would ride home going over the fight. More than likely cursing his name and spitting fire. He could only assume she would've reacted today in the same way.

He half smiled at the knowledge of it. "A stupid thing really. She had agreed with Mr. Tuttle to have Titan cover her mare, Black Lace. By purchasing Titan, that deal is now void. She simply asked me to uphold the agreement, which I refused."

"Why did you refuse?" Duncannon asked. "Was it not your plan to breed Titan and race him? Why not breed with one of the best breeding stables in England? She owns Knight Stables, does she not?"

Tate started toward the house again. "She does, inherited it after her father died twelve months ago."

"So what is the problem?"

The problem was that he was being a stubborn bastard who didn't want to give her what she wished. Not even when she'd asked him so nicely at first. Seeing her again had exacerbated all the injuries of her jilting him. Of wanting something else, books of all things over his love. What type of woman turned down a future duke? Turned her back on the love he'd thought they'd shared? What kind of woman could be so callous with words of sentiments and matters of the heart? A woman who put her own ambition before anything else. And Tate would do the same. With Titan in his stables, the stallion was one step toward becoming real competition to the Knight Stables, to start his own breeding program and produce future horseracing winners. He would not give her the opportunity to best him again, not in business or on a personal level.

"I've changed my mind," he said, shrugging.

"You've changed your mind? Really? Seems to me you're basing your decision on what happened between you all those years ago. Maybe you should accept her offer, but put a stipulation in that should the mare birth a foal that looks promising for racing, any wins the horse might have during its lifetime you'd be entitled to half the profits."

Tate turned to face him. "She'd never agree to such terms. The stables have offered to pay for Titan covering her mare, they will not want to share the profits."

"The stables have bred fifty winners in the last ten years. You could get a piece of the pie. If she wishes for Titan to be used for her breeding program, she'll have to agree," Duncannon said, his business mind coming forth for a moment.

Duncannon was a shrewd man, and some of what he said made sense. It would certainly help financially should the mare breed a winner, and having a horse jointly owned by the renowned Knight Stables would only lift his own name within the racing community.

He thought on the prospect a moment. Ava would not be pleased by this development, and Tate grinned at the idea of annoying her further. If only to see her eyes flash fire at him. "I will think upon it," he said, entering the house. Would think about all the ways he could tell Ava these were his terms and watch the little hellion become further displeased.

Tate pushed the idea away that he'd offer such an idea simply to spend more time with her. She did not deserve his attentions, and yet, walking into his library, Tate's steps were somewhat lighter than when he'd walked out of the room earlier that day. He could not fathom a guess as to why...

CHAPTER 3

*A*s I look out over the French landscape, so very similar and yet different from where we grew up, I wonder if we'll ever see each other again...

— An excerpt from a letter from Miss Ava Knight to the Duke of Whitstone

A week later, Ava lay on her bed, staring down at the unread book in her lap and thinking about a certain duke who had been thrust back into her life.

Three short miles was all that separated them, and yet it wasn't far enough. If only an ocean still kept them apart she would be well pleased. After their disastrous conversation last week, she'd not seen or heard from him. Not that she hoped to, but there was a time when she wouldn't go a day without being near him. If only to tell him how much she had missed him and possibly sneak away for a kiss or two.

Shouts down in the yard caught her attention and dropping the book on the bed, she raced to the window. Ava glanced toward the stables which she could see from her bedroom but couldn't see anything amiss. The men were running toward the barn where the carts were kept, and hearing them yelling orders to grab hessian bags and buckets, fear shot through her that the stables located on the opposite side of her home were on fire.

Ava raced to her closet and pulling on the clothes she'd worn that day, she stumbled into her dressing room, searching for her half boots when she saw an orange glow kiss the night sky. A sickening red radiance coming from the direction of Tate's property.

She stopped for a moment, stunned still at what she could see. Was it the stables or the house? Ava quickly finished dressing, throwing on her boots without stockings.

She ran down the stairs, calling out for the male servants to follow her and within minutes, those who could ride were hard on her heels toward Tate's property, the other men traveling as fast as they could in the carts and buggies.

The closer they came to the ducal estate, the larger the glow in the night sky became, and peeking at the hill she had ridden over only a week before her worst fears were realized. The stables were on fire and the men were fighting the flames, others trying desperately to axe through the side walls of the wooden structure to free the horses.

Leaving the horses in a nearby field, they ran toward the fire, her stable manager handing her a Hessian sack to help. The heat of the fire pricked her flesh as they came up close to it, and wetting the bag in a nearby trough, she started to bash it against the multitude of flames that were licking the wood of several buildings.

Horses were running wild and scared into the night, and all she could hope was that the horses had been spared. The buildings could burn for all she cared, but the life of the horses was paramount.

More shouts sounded from behind her and turning, she saw the second and larger stable catch alight, a pile of straw inside the double frontage doors smoldering and lighting to full flame. She shut her stinging eyes as the smoke blew in her face and opening them again, she could not quite make out who was the man who notified them as he took off in another direction.

"The second stable," she shouted, running toward it. From where she was, Ava could see several horses sticking their heads out over the stall doors inside, looking at the fire, some ran about their stalls, kicking at the walls.

Without thought she ran inside, opening the stall doors as quickly as she could. She covered her mouth with the hessian bag, stumbling and feeling her way along the stalls until she felt the second stall door. Unlocking that too, the horse bolted and sent her flying backwards.

"Ava," she heard Tate's familiar voice yell, and getting to her knees, she blinked as her eyes stung with the smoke that filled the space.

"I'm well. There are more horses back here," she said, getting up and heading toward where she could hear their fear. She would tell the duke after all this, that for a stable to be safe for animals and people, both ends had to have exits. A silly thought at such a time, but nonetheless, she had it. Ava released the last two horses on her side, and raced to the opposite, just as the duke met her at the last stall. He fought with the lock on the door, but it wouldn't budge. "It won't open," he yelled, coughing. "It's locked."

Ava turned about as the flames started to lick the walls of the stall doors opposite them. Looking about she spied an ax on a nearby wall, and running over to it, clasped it. "Here, Tate, use this."

He stared at her a moment, as if she'd grown two heads, before a wooden panel behind them came crashing down and brought him to his senses. "Thank you." He slammed the axe head down once, twice on the door lock and it broke away, allowing them to open the door and free Titan.

The stallion bolted outside, and as they were about to follow the horse, the front of the stable crashed down, trapping them inside.

"Tate," she said, clasping his shirt. "Is there a window or door in this end?" not that she'd seen one, but these were his stables after all, maybe in the smoke and fire she'd not seen any.

"No," he said, pulling her into a nearby stall and shutting the door. Not that it would keep the fire out, but it would halt the straw they were standing on from catching alight before it needed to.

"Stand back, Ava," he said, swinging the axe high and coming down on the stable wall. The smoke grew ever thick and Ava went to the wall, trying to breathe the air that slid between small cracks in the wooden boards. On the outside, she could hear men hitting the wall in the same location that Tate was smashing through. She tried to concentrate on the small amount of fresh air she was breathing, but the heat of the fire on her back made panic settle in her stomach.

"Quick, Tate. I cannot breathe."

A piece of wood smashed in toward them, then more, and with the intrusion of the men outside breaking through, so too did the fresh air. Unfortunately, with the fresh air, the fire behind them only increased its ire.

Her legs refused to move. She tried to crawl over to where there was escape, but her body wouldn't cooperate.

"Ava," Tate said nearby, before she was lifted into familiar, comforting arms. She coughed as he stepped through the hole in the wall, half running, and half stumbling them away from the stable before collapsing on the ground with her in his arms.

She rolled onto the ground, coughing and gasping for breath, and at some point someone passed her a cup of water. Ava turned to see Tate lying beside her, he too was trying to catch his breath. She went over to him and pushed his hair out of his face, waiting for him to meet her eyes.

"Are you well? Are you hurt at all?"

He reached up, running a hand across her cheek. The action brought tears to her eyes that he'd nearly been killed. That they both had. "You look like a chimney sweep."

She laughed despite herself and despite the situation was not at all funny. "You're making jokes, Your Grace? At a time like this," she said, her voice scratchy, her breathing labored, and with a wheeze.

He threw her a mischievous grin. "I think in times like this, amusement is needed." He struggled to sit up and she sat beside him. They were silent a moment as the stable burned before them, the first stable that she had fought to save was nothing now but a charred pile of glowing timber.

The duke's steward came over to them, kneeling down

to their level. "All horses and workers are accounted for, Your Grace. They're in the holding pen down near the house. We're giving them some feed to try and calm them down."

The duke nodded. "Do any of the men know how the fire started? There was no wind, no reason why the second stable would go up like it did."

Ava thought back to hearing shouts behind her when fighting the first fire but the face was as blurry as her sight was right now. "From what I saw, the fire started in the straw that had been piled in the center of the stable after cleaning out the stalls. I heard shouting, as if someone was alerting us to this new threat, but I could not tell you who it was. You don't think it may have been deliberately started, do you?"

And if it had been, where was the culprit? Fear shot through her at the thought. With all her stable hands here fighting the duke's blaze, her own horses were alone at her estate, without protection. She went to stand and Tate's steward pushed her to sit back down.

"Your manager and a couple of your stable hands have headed back to your estate, Miss Knight. I'm sure we would've heard from them should anything be amiss."

Tate sat up beside her and she studied him a moment, glad to see that he seemed to be breathing a little easier.

"We'll have to house the horses somewhere until the stables are gutted and rebuilt. They cannot stay in the fields."

The steward met her gaze, and without asking, she knew what he was hoping. "Of course your stock is welcome to be housed at my stables, Your Grace. There are more than enough stalls for them," she offered, never one to turn away and not help those that were in need.

Even if it was the duke and they were hardly friends. But the horses needed homes and loving the animals as much as she did, she would not leave them out in the cold, even if it were not so very cold at the moment.

"Are you sure, Miss Knight. We have over twenty," the steward said, looking back over to where the horses were standing in the yard and watching the fire burn down what was left of the buildings they'd escaped from.

Ava sighed, watching the horses. "Of course all of them are welcome."

The duke reached out and laid his hand atop hers. Heat, similar to the warmth at her back from the burning stable filled her, and with it a longing for him to touch her like that again. She glanced down at where he'd left his hand and the urge to place hers atop it was almost too much to deny.

Ava met his gaze.

"Thank you," he said, studying her.

She threw him a small smile and, standing, brushed down her breeches and shirt as best as she could.

"I don't think there is much more I can do for you here, and so I'll head back home and let Mr. Brown know that you'll be bringing the horses over for stabling tomorrow."

"Thank you," the Duke said again, looking up from where he sat on the ground, "Truly Ava, thank you."

The steward headed off to oversee elsewhere. Ava turned to take in the devastation of what had happened here tonight. The men still fought to bring the fire to heel, even though it had destroyed all that it had touched. Smoke permeated the air, everyone about them covered in ash and soot, some clothing singed from the flames. "No matter what has passed between us, Your

Grace, I will never turn my back on someone who is in need."

Ava turned and started back to where she had left her mount, hoping the horse would still be there after all the commotion. As it was, a lot of the horses, those that weren't watching the goings-on, were running about the yards, tails high in the air and clearly spooked and uneasy.

The poor souls were lucky to be alive, and if this was a deliberate act of arson, then that would mean everyone in Berkshire were in trouble and would have to be on the lookout.

She'd worked too hard, lost too much already in her life to have it all burned to a cinder due to a fool's desire.

And she would never go down again without a fight.

CHAPTER 4

$\mathcal{T}$he following day Ava was up early, even with the late night before. A few minutes after breakfast, the horses from the duke's estate started to arrive along with their grooms and trainers who would stay and help look after all the horses, to feed, and exercise them daily.

Luckily here at Knight Stables, Ava had her own gallop, and so it was an easy five-minute stroll over to where the horses could go for a run or race.

She sat on the wooden fence that overlooked the yard that her prized breeding mare, Black Lace, was being lunged within. She was a beautiful horse, with her ebony coat and white socks. She hoped the horse would also make beautiful foals.

The mare had good bloodlines, but the horse itself had not had good starts in the few races she had been tried in, and so she was going to breed a foal from her that possibly would. The sire and dam of Black Lace had mixed careers before she retired them both and placed them into her stud program. They had managed one first, but mostly seconds and thirds during their race meets, not great, but also not too terrible either. Such history didn't always mean that the foals of their union would suffer the same fate. If she wanted Knight Stables to survive, she would have to experiment, try expanding and testing breeding theories.

A letter with her father's last wishes had been for her to keep the stables going, to push forward with their plans to make it one of the most prestigious and admired stables in the land. Such a promise had not always been easy to keep, and there were times she was excluded from racing invitations, or her horses were ignored as breeding opportunities simply because she was a woman, but it would not stop her. If anything it had made her more determined to succeed and now nothing would stand in her way of making Knight Stables a household name. As well-known as Tattersalls even, at least in regards to its prized horse stock.

She'd wanted to make a life with Tate all those years ago, leave this life behind, but it was not to quit the racing world in its entirety. Tate and she had simply wanted to make their own stables, become trusted and sought after in their own right. Her father's death had offered her the chance to take over his role, as a woman and an unmarried one at that. She would not let Society's opinions or protocol for a woman to stand in her way and she would not marry simply to make her role here more acceptable, more respectable to the male-dominated world she lived in.

Ava glanced over toward the stables and was glad to see the grooms and stable hands seemed to be greeting each other affably, but even from here she could tell they were tired and in need of a good night's rest, uninterrupted by disaster.

"The duke's coming now, Miss Knight, leading Titan with him," her stable manager said, coming to stand where she sat.

Shading her eyes, Ava looked up on the hill that the duke was riding down. In all the years since she'd seen him, even now his muscular form when atop a horse was on full show and a delight to watch. How well he looked, the years having turned the boy she'd known into a man. A man even she reluctantly agreed was still as handsome as sin.

Ava thought back to the evening before when they had been laying on the ground after escaping the burning stable, the glide of his hand against her cheek when he checked to see if she was well. The look he'd given her had stripped the time away, all the hurts that he'd caused her, and all that she'd cared about in that moment was if he was well, uninjured.

She reached up and touched her cheek, unable to deny that his touch made her yearn for things long buried. He'd been so careful, so kind and gentle that she'd not been able to conceal what he'd always been able to make her feel.

Alive…

Had he noticed her yearning? She could only hope that, in the chaos of last evening, he had not.

"Put Titan in the western stable. It has the larger stalls for horses of his size. He'll be more comfortable there."

"Right away, miss," Greg said, starting toward the duke who had stopped and was talking to both her staff and his own near a watering trough.

He glanced over to her and nodded in acknowledgement and Ava did the same before turning her attention back to her mare who continued to lunge in a canter.

She supposed she would have to go, speak to him, and discuss his own sleeping arrangement now that all his horses were here. Knowing the duke as she did, she did not think he'd want to return to his estate. Not that she could offer him a bed under her roof, being unmarried and without a chaperone as she was. But there was a cottage that she'd had refurbished the previous year that sat down near the natural running stream on the property, and wasn't far from the stables.

The duke could stay there and still be close enough to keep an eye on his horses and the continuation of their training while his own stables were rebuilt.

"Wash Black Lace after her workout and ensure she gets a good rubdown. I think she's earned her oats this evening."

The stable hand dipped his hat and pulled Black Lace into a trot.

Ava jumped down and started toward the western stable. No time like the present to discuss how they would go on, now that the duke was here. By the time she'd walked over to the stable, the duke and Titan had disappeared into the building. She went inside and coming up to the stall where Titan was standing, patted the stallion as he came over to her and nudged her hand.

"He likes you," the duke said, coming to stand beside her, a biscuit of hay in his hand. He reached over the stable door and placed it in the feed bin.

With food on offer, Titan left her and went to nibble on his hay. "He's such a beautiful horse and loving, by the looks of it. Spoiled perhaps," she said, grinning at the duke who smiled back. Oh, how she'd missed that smile...

"I do spoil him, and he's settled in quite well at home, or at least he had until the fire. I'm not sure what type of issues we may have, going forward, with the horses being frightened so much last night. Some of the mares may miscarry."

Ava nodded, knowing only too well that horses could

be easily spooked after such a traumatic event. She could only hope that it wasn't the case with any of the duke's horses. "They'll soon settle and know they're quite safe here, and I've instructed my stable hands to take shifts in watching the stables and barns about the property."

"I have sent for a Bow Street Runner to look into the fire at the Hall. I cannot help but think it was deliberately started."

Ava remembered back to the man who shouted out behind her, notifying them of another fire. Was that the man who'd started such destruction and if so, why. Why would anyone wish to hurt horses that were locked away in stalls and defenseless against such actions?

"Do you have any idea who may wish to injure you and your horses? Have you quarreled with anyone of late?" she asked, meeting his gaze.

The duke threw her an amused glance. "Other than you, no one."

She chuckled at his attempt of a joke and reached into the stall to run her finger across Titan's shoulder. "Well you know I would never do such a thing, so someone has a grudge against you, Your Grace. You need to find out whom?"

"Hmm," he said, turning about to lean against the stable door and crossing his arms against his chest.

She glanced back at the horse, as the action only accentuated the muscles on Tate's chest. Oh yes, he'd changed and for the delectable better.

"I did have to let go of a stable lad who'd become too close to a maid in the house, had started to harass her somewhat and was trying for liberties that were not his to have. It could be him, I suppose, but I have not seen or heard he's still in Berkshire working elsewhere, so I do doubt that is a lead."

"I would tell the Runner in any case, and let him look into any tips. In this business, we may be civil and act as if racing is a gentleman's sport, but really, we all have many enemies, jealousy being the foremost." Lord Oakes flittered through Ava's mind at the mention of jealousy, and she dismissed the notion instantly that he might have been involved.

He wouldn't dare.

"I would've thought your stables to be in more danger than mine on that score. Yours have certainly won more races recently than mine. I did fear, when everyone was fighting the fires at the Hall, that your own livelihood might also be at risk."

It was a fear that Ava had herself, and thankfully her stables and horses had been fine upon their return. To think of losing the animals which she loved so dearly, who had been her company and salvation through so many troubles in her life, filled her with dread. If what the duke was saying was true, then they needed to find the culprit and have him thrown away into a cell where he couldn't hurt anything or anyone again.

"When I saw the glow of the fire at your estate, I did not even think to leave someone here to keep an eye on my horses. A foolish mistake I'll not make again. We are very thankful that none here were put in harm's way. And we're happy that your horses are here too. It will give me time to convince you to allow me to breed Titan with Black Lace."

At the mention of the horse's name, the stallion lifted his head out of his feed bin and glanced in their direction. Ava laughed, reaching out to pat the horse's soft velvety nose. "What a mischief maker you are," she cooed to the horse, overlooking for a moment the duke was still beside her.

"I forgot this." He glanced down at her and Ava fought not to meet his gaze. To become lost once again in his dark, gray orbs that were like a stormy, swirling sea.

"Forgot what, Your Grace?" She shouldn't ask, but where the duke was involved, there was little she could do to stop herself. Like a moth drawn to the hottest part of the flame, so too was she drawn to hearing what he wanted to say about them. About their past, when the only things worth fighting for were each other.

"How you were with horses. How much you love them."

"I do adore them." She sighed, stepping back from the stall. "But it was not all that I loved."

"You're still reading gothic novels then, and sneaking out in the middle of the night to count the stars?" he asked, smiling.

Warmth spread through her, comforting and familiar, that the man before her knew her as well as anyone in the world. "Of course, although I no longer have to sneak out, I can simply walk out the front door."

"True," he said, glancing at the blue sky above them. "Do you remember when we met down by the lake on my property in the dead of night? You were so determined to draw the full moon that I almost froze to death waiting for you to sketch it."

"I'll have you know that my father, even though he never questioned me as to how I came to own such a sketch, was very fond of that drawing. He even framed it. It hangs in the library." Ava sighed, thinking on that night. It had been the first time they had kissed, not as an

45

acquaintance and friend, but as lovers, as a couple who longed for more than mere familiarity.

Meeting the duke's gaze, the banked fire she read in his eyes told her he remembered the night as well as she did. Ava cleared her throat. "We should probably discuss what you're going to do now that all your horses are here. I have a cottage that I've recently repaired that is separate from the staff quarters, but it's still close enough to see the horse yards, barns and stables if you wanted it. I would invite you, of course, to stay at the main house, but well, as you know that wouldn't be proper."

His eyes darkened at the mention of the word proper and what her meaning implied. "Is that the old cottage where your cook, Mrs. Gill, used to reside?"

"Yes, that's right. She left our employment some years ago, and the new cook preferred to stay at the main house." She started toward the stable doors. "Come, I'll walk you down there now and you can decide if it'll suit."

They made their way through the yards, walking across the meadow that sat at the back of her home, and they soon came to the small cottage that sat overlooking the stream. Ava turned and gestured toward the view. "Here, you can see the entire layout of the property, except the front of the main house."

He took in the situation and nodded. "This will do very well." He turned back to her. "What happened to Mrs. Gill. I always adored her—"

"Rout cakes?" Ava answered for him. "Yes, I remember." Ignoring the familiarity they had. She opened the door to the cottage and stepped inside the three-room home. "Her daughter who worked for a family in Kent married a baker and offered her mother a place with them.

Mrs. Gill lived with her daughter for two years or so, but became ill last autumn and sadly passed away."

"I'm sorry to hear that. She was a lovely woman, much liked by the staff, from what I can remember."

Ava smiled, thinking back. "She was lovely and is sorely missed. I do not believe the rout cakes have ever tasted as good as when she was here."

The duke ducked through the doorway and inspected the modest kitchen, the bedroom and washroom that ran off of it. Ava considered him for a moment, having forgotten how well they had known each other. How much time they had spent in each other's company over the years.

The cottage was tidy, with wooden flooring, a large woven mat sitting beneath the small table that was placed not far from the fire. In the bedroom there was a large unmade bed, along with a small window with blue velvet curtains. The washroom comprised a jug and bowl, a washstand, a small hip bath and chamber pot that sat on the floor.

"This will do very well, thank you."

"I'll have the maids come through and make up the bed daily and get you some fresh linens and water. Of course, you do not have to eat here, you're more than welcome to dine with me each night and break your fast in the morning at the main house." Ava wasn't sure where her failure to leave him well alone and keep their distance came from. The duke did not fit in with her plans for the future. For years, she'd schooled herself to move on, to not need his opinion or support. The fire and smoke inhalation had obviously muddled her mind.

Ava shut her mouth with a snap and busied herself inspecting the oven. She was being too kind to the duke, and they were not even on the best of terms with each other. Why was she going out of her way for him? A terrible little voice whispered it was because she still cared for him, even after all this time and all the pain he'd caused her.

Taking one last inspection of the cottage, she started toward the door. "I'll leave you to it," she said, not taking one step before he clasped her arm, halting her.

"Truly, thank you Ava, not just for taking my horses or giving me leave to use this cottage, but for last night. For coming to my aid, not leaving my side or my horses, when by staying, put you in extreme danger. I shall not forget your kindness."

She stepped away from his hold, not liking the fact that her body refused to remain indifferent to him and his touch. If they were to be on the same property with each other for some weeks, she had best start to learn to be around the duke and not show her emotions like an open book waiting to be read.

"It was nothing, Your Grace. Nothing that you, yourself, would not do for me in return, I'm sure." She started toward her home, needing to get away from the expression of devotion that was written all over his visage. The last thing she needed was for him to start looking at her in such a way. The way he used to when they were young.

～

*T*ate leaned against the doorframe of his cottage as Ava strode back to her home. With her wearing breeches, not a dress, it gave him the perfect opportunity to admire her from behind. He fisted his hands at his sides, as longing for what was lost washed over him like water.

Had he stayed, had she not rejected him all those years ago, they would be married by now. Possibly even be parents and raising their children to take over the great racing estate they wanted to forge on their own. To have a son who would inherit his title and maybe if blessed, a daughter who would be as wild and unmanageable as her mama.

He closed the door and leaned against it. He didn't have to stay at Knight Stables, but the thought of going back to the Hall did not appeal to him either. His horses were here, and he could have his steward send his paperwork over regarding his estates. If what his stable manager had said this morning was right and the evidence he'd found in the rubble of the fires was correct, there was an arsonist on the run.

It was best he was near Ava in case she was the fiend's next victim. His steward would keep watch of Cleremore Hall until the stables were rebuilt and he could return. In truth, he was here at Ava's home because this was where she was and now that they were at least on pleasant turns with each other, he was loath to leave.

She'd always had the ability to draw him in. Make him long even to hear her voice or see her across a field. Tate pushed away from the door and opened it, needing to tell his valet where to bring his bags. At least, such a task would keep his mind occupied for a time and not so obsessed with a woman who'd ripped his heart out of his chest that felt like only yesterday.

CHAPTER 5

I have no hopes that we can be anything other than passing acquaintances in the future, but know that I shall always care for you. That you were my friend and will always be part of me.

— An excerpt from a letter from Miss Ava Knight to the Duke of Whitstone

The next month kept everyone busy at both Ava's farm and the rebuilding of the duke's stables at his own estate. A couple of times, Tate had asked her for an opinion on the layout and design of the new stalls and stables, and together they had come up with what would be modern and practical solutions to any issues they'd had in the past.

And most importantly, the stables were brick instead of wood and all would be built with a second access door in case one is blocked, as what happened at the fire.

Ava sat behind her desk in the library and leaned back

in her chair, looking out over the grounds. The day had come in stormy and so a lot of the activities she'd had planned for the day had been put off until tomorrow.

She stood and walked over to the window, looking in the direction of the small cottage that the duke had made his own these past weeks. Most nights he came to dine with her and, unfortunately with each night, Ava was reminded of what could have been. Of what she had lost when Tate had chosen a different path than the one they had planned.

They had not spoken of what had happened between them, in fact, they both seemed to be at pains to never bring up their past. She did not mention France and he did not mention New York. It was no surprise that they could not go on in such a way. There was a glaringly taboo subject they needed to talk about. Ava especially needed to know why. Just why he'd lied and not loved her as she'd thought he had.

How he thought that after all the time they'd spent together, she only deserved a letter to tell her all her dreams were crushed. A letter delivered to her father, not even herself. Why could he not have done the deed himself?

With the rain pelting against the window pane, the small glow of candlelight at the cottage became blurred, a small wisp of smoke floated into the sky from the chimney. Dinner was not so very far away and then he would arrive...

She turned and started for her room, bathed quickly, then had her maid help her dress. Most days she wore men's breeches, paid little attention to her hair or how clean her boots were. But tonight she would wear one of the new gowns she'd ordered from London when she'd traveled there last month to ensure her manager had purchased a yearling from Tattersalls she'd wanted. Madame Lanchester had accommodated her without trouble and her abilities as a seamstress were better than Ava had hoped.

Over the years they had been apart, the thought had crossed her mind more than once that the reasoning behind the duke's crying off their elopement had been because she was too rough about the edges. Not ladylike enough or educated in the arts of a lady as most duchesses would be. For months she'd lain awake, wondering if her wearing of breeches, and unfashionable straw bonnets had put him off. That, in time, he'd come to realize himself that she would never make a good duchess.

Which was perfectly correct, she would not, not now at least, too much had happened in the five years since they'd parted. She was certainly no duchess material now, but that did not mean for herself she could not dress up, show the duke that one ought to look past the outer shell of a person to what they were inside. Maybe he'd forgotten what it was that had drawn him to her in the first place.

Ava stared at herself in the mirror. Her embroidered muslin shift was simply the prettiest undergarment she owned and it was almost too pretty to cover up with a dress.

"Which gown, Miss Ava, would you like to wear?" Her maid opened the armoire and started inspecting the few gowns that she owned.

"The bronze silk with lace and pearl edging, and I'd like my hair placed in soft curls atop my head, if you can tonight, Jane."

Her maid smiled, busying herself preparing the gown. "Oh, you'll look lovely this evening, Miss Ava. And I've been practicing with some new French designs for your hair. It'll look right pretty with the cut of the dress."

Which, Ava had to admit, looking over the gown lying on her bed was very low about the breast. A delicate lighter bronze ribbon ran beneath the chest line, and a delicate fleur-de-lis pattern in pearl and silk lace ran along the hem.

"Thank you, Jane." Ava smiled at her maid, eager for the night to commence.

Over the next hour Jane fussed with Ava's hair, pulling it up into a semblance of style, not simply tied back with a ribbon that she always sported, and she was ready for dinner.

The sound of male voices came from downstairs and Ava caught her maid's eye. "I'll go downstairs, Miss Ava, and tell the kitchen staff to start serving upon your arrival downstairs."

"Thank you, Jane." Ava turned back to the mirror and studied her appearance. Her maid had done wonders with her hair and somehow the woman who trained racehorses, wore breeches and mucked out stables as well as any of her staff had vanished. Instead, reflecting back at her was a woman who was the master of her own life. Tate had broken her heart, he had not broken her spirit. And the little devil in her wanted to show him what he'd lost. What he would never have again.

Winking at herself, she grinned and turned to leave, snatching up her shawl, laying it across her shoulders. The dress shimmied about her, cool and soft, and she had the overwhelming feeling of being almost naked.

It had been so long since she'd been to a ball or party, or even dressed up for dinner. Here at home she never followed the strict rules of the *ton*, and she supposed it could be one of the reasons Tate had fled to America instead of marrying her.

Ava checked her gown as she made the stairs, and her steps faltered at the vision Tate made waiting for her at the bottom. Gone were his tan breeches, and soiled shirt she'd seen him in over the last few weeks. Gone was the man who exercised the horses, helped build his new stables, and ran about both her and his own estate daily keeping up with all that he had to. Ruffled, dusty or muddy depending on the English weather.

Before her stood a duke. The boy she'd loved and the man she'd come to respect in a lot of ways again. In his buckskin trousers and glistening black knee-high boots, his silver waistcoat, his perfectly starched shirt and tied cravat. Well, words failed her a moment.

Never had she thought he could become more attractive than he did right at this moment. She had pictured him dressed so when imagining their Gretna Green wedding, before he hightailed it to America. She pushed the thought aside, not wanting it to dampen her mood.

She moved off the last step, and he dipped his head a little in greeting, but not before she saw the flare of awareness that entered his eyes.

Did he like what he saw too? Did he regret his choice? Ava, at least, certainly hoped so.

～

Tate took the opportunity, as he bowed to Ava, to school his features to one of indifference and not what he really felt each and every time he saw the woman before him. The overwhelming desire to fall to his knees and ask her to tell him why she'd turned away from his love all those years ago.

She'd not married, which was the first thing he had expected to hear while away in America, but no such news had reached him and it only muddled his mind with the need to know the truth. Why did she not love him anymore? Why had she sent him that cold, unfeeling letter the night before their elopement.

His parents had only gone so far as to update him that she was away at school and seemingly enjoying the continent immensely, not missing her home or those she left behind. The change in her character had been so altered from the Ava he'd known, that he couldn't help but wonder if it were true. Could people really be so false?

He gestured for her to take his arm to walk her into the dining room. The intoxicating scent of roses filled the air and left him with a longing for a time long past. He closed his eyes a moment to compose himself.

How a scent could bring back so many memories he'd never understand, but it did.

She sat herself down at the table, and he took in her silk gown that was adorned with lace and gold thread. The gown was the height of fashion, and her figure was most pleasing within it. Gone was the body of a girl on the brink of womanhood. Seated across from him was a woman who would please even the starchiest of men.

Her long russet brown locks were pulled back into a delicate coil of curls, accentuating her perfect shoulders and neck. Her eyes, wide and clear, sparkled with pleasure and her lips shone with the lightest touch of rouge, and playfully quirked into a smile. Seeing Ava tonight, feminine and all soft curves, hell and damnation, she was beautiful.

A nearby servant poured them glasses of wine and taking his seat, Tate waited for the first course to be served.

Ava adjusted her seat, placing the napkin on her lap before meeting his gaze over the highly polished mahogany table.

"Thank you for coming tonight, I did wonder if you would since the weather has been dreadful today..." her words trailed off as a hot, steaming vegetable soup was placed before them.

"I do not mind the walk, although with the rain this evening I was grateful for the carriage Mr. Brown sent for me. As short as the ride was, it made the hike a lot less wet underfoot." Tate almost rolled his eyes at the banal conversation. There was a time when they would share every thought, dream and desire. That they had lost their way, lost each other, maddened him. He frowned, turning to a servant.

"Wine for us both. Thank you."

The young man bowed, quickly going about his duties. "Yes, Your Grace."

Tate waited for the wine to be poured. "We will call when we're ready for the next course. Thank you," he said to the servants, not speaking again until they had all shuffled out the room and he and Ava were alone.

Finally...

"There is something that I wish to discuss with you, Ava and it's probably best that this subject is discussed while we're alone. And forgive me, but I cannot wait any longer to know what has been vexing me for quite some time."

She looked at him wide-eyed, and placed down her glass of wine after taking a sip. "Of course. What is it you wish to say?"

He leaned back in his chair, idly playing with his soup with the spoon. After a time, he willed himself to speak the words that had been locked inside him for too many years. "Why did you not elope with me?"

She laid down her spoon, her face ashen. "Why did I not elope with you?" She laughed the sound mocking. "Are you really asking me that question?"

He nodded, once. "Why?"

Ava studied him a moment and he could see her trying to understand why he was asking such a question after all these years. But if he didn't know the truth behind her decision, it would continue to drive him mad.

"I snuck out of the house in the middle of the night and made my way to our tree. You were not there, but my father was. He informed me that you'd left for London where you were catching a ship to America. He said that you had written and cried off, saying that the under-standing that you believed I harbored was a mistake. That I was hoping for a connection that would never eventuate being that you were heir to a dukedom and we were not a family with connections or nobility."

A punch to his gut would've caused less pain. Tate thought back to that night and the situation that led to his parents coming into his room.

He'd been packing not five minutes before and had been thankful that they had not seen his small luggage case that was sitting in his dressing room. His mother had sat before the fire on the leatherback chair he'd often read in, his father standing behind her.

Tate reached into his coat pocket and pulled out the missive that they had handed to him, having retrieved it earlier that day from his ducal estate, determined to find out the reason behind their parting.

He handed it to Ava, and she reached across, taking it without question before unfolding it and reading the note.

Horror crossed her features.

"I, ah…" she bit her lip, gasping as she read the last of the note. "I didn't write this, Tate." She looked up at him, shock etched on her sweet visage. "Our parents must have worked together on keeping us apart. My father," she paused, her eyes welling with tears. "I cannot believe he would hurt me in such a way." For a moment they stared at each other in silence before she said, "I can only gather from this that the letter your father sent per your favor was not from you either." She refolded the letter, sliding it across the table to him. "I do not have your father's letter on me, but I have kept it. I will show it to you tomorrow."

"I need to see it now," he demanded, pushing back his chair to stand. He went around the table and helped Ava out of her seat and, taking her hand, pulled her toward the dining room door. It had been years since he'd touched her in such a way. To have her silk-gloved hand within his own brought back all the longing that he'd had to endure knowing she didn't want him. A lie that he now believed his parents had fabricated.

A lie he would travel to London and ask his mother about and see if she could explain her despicable actions.

He wrenched the door open and the footmen who waited for instruction started, standing to attention.

She'd not scorned him. Did that mean she'd been as heartbroken as he had been all these years without her? The memory of how he'd tried to forget her. The many women he'd bedded, had on call for his desires, all a distraction for a heart that called out for another thought lost. How would he ever make it up to her…?

Entering the hall, they quickly made their way upstairs.

Tate ignored the shocked and inquisitive glances from the staff who viewed an unmarried woman lead a duke into her private quarters.

He didn't give a damn about what proprieties he was breaking. The anger that thrummed through his veins at what their parents had done, pushed away any thought of what was right and wrong at this present moment.

She came to a room at the end of the hall and, casting him a nervous glance, entered.

Tate leaned against the door's threshold, not willing to completely breach her private space and yet, for the first time, he glimpsed into her most private of places; her bedroom. Where he'd imagined a more masculine feel for a woman who rode horses and mucked out stables like the best stable lad in Berkshire, her room was all soft tones of blue and pink. The furniture was white and looking about it reminded Tate of a field of flowers on a summer's day.

Ava walked over to a small bedside cabinet and opening the drawer, pulled out a folded missive. She came back to him, handing it over.

He opened and scanned the note quickly. His stomach churned. His mother's writing. So she had been involved in this scheme to separate them, a scheme that had worked for too many years. But no longer. Not if Ava would have him back.

"My mother's writing, I'm afraid." He folded it and handed it back to her. "I don't know what to say other than I'm sorry, Ava. I did not think our families could be so cruel as to play such a trick on us both, but alas, it seems that is what has happened."

She walked slowly over to her bed and sat on its edge. "I said to papa, on the night he told me that you were not going to arrive, that he was wrong. That you would come because it was so out of character for you. I could not believe that the boy I loved could play such a cruel joke on me. Lie to my face about what he supposedly felt for me, only to turn about and say it was all in my imagination."

He went over to her and knelt, taking her hand. "I could not do that to you because I did not do this to you. Our families did this to us. I'm sorry Ava and I promise you that I'll find out why."

Tate had a small idea as to why his parents disapproved of Ava. Their social standing was as different as the horses' temperaments they owned between them. His mother had never approved of their friendship and, now that these letters and who was actually behind them had been revealed, he would confront his mother and demand an apology. One for himself and one for Ava. He was no longer the Marquess, he was now the duke, and he would damn well marry whomever he pleased.

She squeezed his hand in return. "As much as this shocks me, Tate, I'm glad we know the truth and we can go on without any animosity between us."

The years fell away and he wanted to take her in his arms, surround himself with the smell of roses that always permeated the air around Ava. Certainly, he didn't want any animosity between them to continue, but he also didn't wish for them to be distant. Ava had once been his best friend, his heart, and he would give anything to win her back.

She pulled her hand free and he stood, giving her space.

"You should probably leave. We both have a lot to think about. I'm sorry to cut our dinner short, but I think its best."

"Of course," he said, heading for the door. "I will bid

you goodnight." Tate closed the door behind him and leaned on it a moment to catch his breath. It was hard to know what to do from here, how to begin again. As young as they both had been when they'd both declared their love, and it had been love, true and as pure as air they breathed. A lot of things had happened since, a lot of time had passed. His own life in London wasn't something he was proud of. He cringed knowing news of his antics had reached Berkshire and Ava. He'd been a distant landlord after his father passed, wishing to bury himself in the amusements of London than to grow up and return home, take up his role as he should have. All because he was angry, not just at himself, but at the cards life had dealt him regarding Ava.

Tate started for the stairs, needing to return to his estate to organize travel to London. He needed to return to town and confront his mother over her cruel meddling in his life which meant he had lost the one woman who truly knew and loved him for him, not who he was or what he offered.

He clenched his jaw. Due to his earlier careless actions, his trip to town would also mean he would have to visit his leman, not that anyone knew such a thing about him, and part ways from her. The confrontation might not go well and he would have to provide a monetary lump sum for the congé.

Then, he could return to Berkshire and win back his lady. His duchess, as Ava always should have been.

CHAPTER 6

fter sending a missive to Ava, telling her of his
plans to travel to town, he arrived in London late
the following day just as the little season was starting. Tate
jumped down from his carriage as the lamplighters walked
the streets and lit the pavement lamps.

Tate went straight round to Whites to catch up with his
good friend, Lord Duncannon, whom he'd asked last
month to return to London to hire a Bow Street Runner,
even though for the past month there had been little
evidence come to light nor any further attacks on the
estates other than his own.

He went into the foyer and before a footman could take
his coat, he was handed a missive from Lord Duncannon
telling him he'd been held up elsewhere and would be
joining him later than they'd planned.

Tate turned and stared out toward the street, debating
with himself if he could put off seeing the woman who'd
warmed his bed regularly during the past year in town.
Having sent a missive the previous day of his impending
arrival, he knew his arrival would be met with her

believing all was well and expecting a night of passion would commence.

Girding his loins, he left, calling out the road to his driver and hating himself for the fact that he was going to hurt her. Fleur, Lady Clapham and the widow to Viscount Clapham, did not deserve such treatment. Not that she had ever aspired to be his wife, but he had promised not to make a fool of her in Society, and they were often seen together at events and balls. She had been a friend, a comfort during his flashes of weakness and the loneliness that had plagued him sporadically since arriving back in England.

The carriage rocked to a halt before the portland stone townhouse in Mayfair and he stared at the building a moment before his groom opened the door. Tate jumped down and walked up the stairs. The butler let him in without question or delay, and automatically Tate started toward the front parlor where Fleur always liked to meet prior to their rendezvous.

The parlor was his least favorite room in the home, having been decorated in the most vile shade of pink that hurt one's eyes.

The butler opened and shut the door without comment, and taking a step further into the room, Tate couldn't help but smile at the pose Fleur had positioned herself in as she awaited his arrival.

Her ladyship was sprawled on a pink settee, one arm lazily lying behind her head while the other sat atop her stomach that was visible through the transparent silk shift she wore. Her nipples, a pink that suited her surroundings, stood erect beneath her garment, and the darker patch of curls at the apex of her thighs was visible.

Even with the knowledge that he would never have the

woman in the way she expected again, he could not deny that she was beautiful and deserving of so much more than life had given her, himself included. Her father, a country gentleman had fallen on hard times, and with his downfall, so too had his children. Lady Clapham had been married off to a rich viscount without a moment's thought. It was now left on her shoulders to support her siblings and find grand matches when their times came, and so Lady Clapham had married a man twice her age and with a rumored temper as hot as Hades.

"Tate, my darling, where have you been? The little season is almost over, and we have not seen you these past months. I truly despaired that you would never return to town again. I've been so lonely," she said, her gaze raking him with unsated lust.

He sat on a chair opposite her, and sensing that he wasn't going to sit beside her and take her in his arms, Fleur sat up, pulling her dressing gown about her front. "Is something the matter?" she asked.

"There is something that I need to speak to you about and I'm afraid that you may not like what it is." If he knew Fleur at all, and he did, very well, she was not a woman to cross and he didn't want for them to part on bad terms. What they had was enjoyable while it lasted, but he'd never given her false hope. Had never offered more than what they had agreed to before any liaison had started.

"I'm going to be spending a great deal of time in Berkshire, at my estate. As you may be aware, there was a fire at my stables last month—"

Fleur gasped, leaning forward. "There was a fire? Was there much damage?"

"I lost two stable blocks that I'm in the process of rebuilding. All my horses have had to be stabled at

Knight's. I was extremely fortunate not to lose any of my cattle."

The viscountess leaned back in her chair, a knowing look in her eyes. "Is not Knight Stables owned by Miss Ava Knight? Was she not the girl who jilted you all those years ago?"

Tate didn't want to tell Fleur the whole truth, for as soon as he did the whole of London would know and no one here in town needed to have any participation in his life.

"She's home from France and is doing an excellent job keeping her racing stables profitable and successful. What happened in the past between us I'd prefer to leave in the past. We are neighbors, and due to our mutual love of horseracing, we need to get along."

"Well," she said, her tone having a disbelieving edge to it. "I'm glad you've been able to put the past behind you, but that does not mean that we cannot still be together when you're in town. We get along well enough, and you know we always have fun. Do not be a bore and tell me that we can no longer go on as we have been."

Tate was gambling on the idea that in time and with patience, he could possibly win Ava's love back. Make her see that together they could make both their estates the best racing and breeding stables in the land. That under no circumstances would he try to clip her wings and force her to change, to suit his title. They had both longed for children, and a marriage built on a strong foundation of love. He would not give up on such hopes now that the possibility of them was perhaps an option once again.

He stood. "I'm sorry, Fleur, but I can no longer be your lover. I will, of course, always be your friend and should you need anything at all, you know that I will always offer assistance. But what we've had must come to an end. It would not be fair to you to keep you for myself when we've always been in agreement that this was only ever temporary and a fun way to pass the time during the Season."

She studied him a moment before she stood, coming up to him and wrapping her arms about his neck. "I shall miss you, Your Grace, and all the delectable things we used to get up to. I look forward to seeing you next year in town."

Tate untangled her arms from about his neck, but leaned down and kissed her quickly on the brow. "Good night, Lady Clapham." He handed her the congé.

He left without another word, and reaching his carriage called for Whites. Lady Clapham had taken the news much better than he'd thought she would have. Perhaps she already had someone else in mind to keep her occupied. She was a widow and many gentlemen had taken an interest in her, which she was always amenable to.

And now they were both free to do as they pleased. And it pleased Tate very well to win Ava's love. He'd won her heart once before, surely that meant he could do it again.

CHAPTER 7

wo years have passed since I saw you last. Sometimes I wonder if we shall ever meet again...

— An Excerpt from a letter from Miss Ava Knight to the Duke of
Whitstone

ate's carriage pulled up before his London townhouse, the lights blazing from within and the sound of music playing made his steps cautionary as he walked up to the front door. A footman in red livery, clothing that they only used when hosting a ball, made his steps falter. Of all the days he would return to London would be one of the days that his mother was hosting a party.

This would make it the third for the year. Did the woman not have anything better to do with her time? He handed his great coat to one of the servants that came upon him in the entrance hall and said hello to the few people who mingled outside the ballroom.

Not in the mood for such entertainments, he started up the stairs. Not only did he not want to socialize, but he was far from dressed for a ball. Come morning, he would discuss his mother's excessive hosting and try and rein her in a little. Not to mention the letter she wrote to Ava being foremost in his mind made him less than willing to allow her little follies.

Halfway up the stairs a gentleman's voice yelled out to him and Tate paused, turning to see the Earl of Brandon, his good friend whom he'd met during his first year in New York.

"Scott," he said, coming down the stairs and pulling him into an embrace. The man was one of his closest friends, and he'd missed him when he'd left to return home to England. Scott had traveled to England as well, but had gone on to Europe to see the sights. "How have you been, my friend?"

"Very well. Very well, indeed," Scott said, grinning. "I remembered the dowager duchess was holding a ball tonight to bid farewell to the little season and thought to catch up with you while you were in town."

"May I say congratulations? I will admit to being quite surprised when receiving your letter that you were engaged, but I'm happy for you. Is your betrothed with you? I would love to meet her," Tate said, glancing about to see if any one young lady was waiting to be called over for an introduction.

"Yes, you are right. I'm engaged. We're to marry next June. Her family will be traveling over from Italy as they wish to prepare and plan the wedding with Rosa. Of course, I'm all for allowing Rosa to have whatever she wants."

Tate smiled. "I'm happy for you, my friend. You will make a wonderful husband and I am sure Rosa will make you a wonderful wife if she's the one you've chosen. I count the days until I can meet her."

"They're on their way now from Rome and will arrive by Christmas. I will be sure to introduce you. She is simply perfect."

Tate clasped him on the shoulder, happy for his friend. "You're a good man. You deserve this bliss."

"Thank you," Scott said, turning toward the ballroom. "Shall we have a glass of champagne to celebrate?"

Tate could not refuse and so started toward the ballroom doors. In no way was he dressed for the occasion, but being the Duke of Whitstone did give him some leave to wear whatever he damn well pleased.

He caught sight of his mother across the other side of the ballroom, her eyes widening in shock. Tate wasn't sure if it was because he was here, or because of what he was wearing, possibly both.

Scott took two glasses of champagne from a passing footman and handed one to Tate. They made the congratulatory toast and took a sip before looking about.

"When are you returning to Berkshire. I heard from Duncannon that you've had some troubles at the Hall."

Tate nodded. The mention of home brought up the memory of Ava and how much he missed seeing her, even for a day. He had become accustomed to being near her again, and now that he was in town, he itched to rid himself of the city and get back to the country. How he had put up with living here for the past two years, never leaving for the country, was beyond him.

"I have some business to attend to here, but no more than a week, and I'll return to Berkshire. As for the trouble, yes, I've had some of late."

The Earl gave him his full attention and Tate debated whether to tell Scott all he was thinking. They had never held anything back from each other before and Tate could not do so now. He needed to discuss Ava with someone or he'd go mad. "Do you remember a lady I once spoke to you about, and the reason why I was in America in the first place?"

Scott nodded. "Of course. Miss Knight, was it not?"

"Yes, that's right," Tate said, warmth seeping through his veins at the mention of her name aloud.

"She lives in France I understand, but her father owned one of the best racehorse stables in England."

"Yes, you remember correctly, but alas, she's not in France. She's back in Berkshire."

His friend studied him a moment before he raised his brow, his mouth twitching in amusement. "She's returned? How very interesting." He paused. "And does this have anything to do with why you're now living in Berkshire instead of London?"

"Not entirely," Tate said, not wanting to look like too much of a lovesick puppy, but then he'd never been able to lie to Scott. "I will disappoint you in telling you our reunion was not my finest hour, but then as you may have heard my stable block was burned down, which I will go into later with you, but on that night, Ava saved my prized stallion and me to an extent."

"And so you've formed a truce."

Tate shrugged. "I have had to move my horses over to her estate, and over the last month, since the fire, we've come to know that she never jilted me five years ago. In fact, both our parents played us for fools and removed us from the other's life. It is also another reason why I'm in town. I want to confront my mother about her involvement in such an underhanded scheme."

Scott whistled, his eyes wide. "The dowager never approved of Miss Knight. Did you know?"

"Mother never said such a thing to me directly, the letter, which I've read is in her hand. Her distaste for Miss Knight as my wife was clear in every word. I did not think her capable of such treachery, but I was wrong. It was no wonder Ava never reached out to me over the years. The letter was very cold and offensive."

Tate shook his head, hating that they'd been ripped apart all because someone else thought it best for them. "We had dinner the other evening and during the conversation, I could not stand not knowing the truth as to what happened. Why she sent me the note crying off our understanding. It was then that she asked about my letter in turn. Both of which neither of us had written. We had both been played and by the people we were supposed to trust most." Tate looked across the room and watched his mother a moment with her friends, laughing and lording it over others simply because she was a duchess. A cold, hard lump formed in his gut and he turned back to Scott, not wanting to look a moment longer.

"I've returned to town in part to confront my mother about her despicable actions. I had meant to do it tonight, but returning home I found she's hosting this ball, so our conversation will have to wait until the morning."

"What other business brings you here?" his friend asked.

Tate adjusted his cravat and cleared his throat. "Well, other than some business in town regarding my other estates, and my issue with my mother of course, the other reason I was back in town was because of a delicate subject."

Scott raised his brow. "Really, care to elaborate?" His friend finished his champagne and summoned more from a footman nearby.

Tate ground his teeth, not liking the fact he'd succumbed like so many men of his sphere and taken a lover. Lady Clapham had not been his mistress, she was free to do whatever she like and with whomever she choose, the fact he could call on her when it pleased him, did make her seem like a mistress, although he did not want to use that term.

He glanced about to ensure they were not within hearing of nearby guests. "Not my finest hour, but I have been sleeping with a woman this past year. No one knows, and I'm sure she took other lovers during that time, but if I want any sort of future with Miss Knight, I had to be honest with her. I just came from her home here in Mayfair."

"Did she take the news well?"

Better than Tate had thought she would, but then they both had always been honest and Lady Clapham had said many times that she did not want to marry again. "She did. In fact, she was hardly bothered at all." A lucky escape if Tate was being honest with himself. Lady Clapham was a complex woman and one never knew which way she could twist.

He sighed. "Even tying up all my loose ends may serve me very little. I'm no longer certain that Miss Knight will have me. After finding out the truth, she remained distant." Tate ran a hand through his hair, unsure what Ava felt. "It did not seem like she was sure any longer what she wanted in life, whether she wanted me or not."

"How so?" Scott asked.

"I've come to think she no longer wishes for that institution to be part of her life. She is so very independent, runs her racing estate with expert precision, is thorough and fair, and is beholden to no one. Becoming a duchess brings with it new responsibilities and pressure, and I'm not sure she has room for that in her life." There was a time when she'd not wanted anything else but to be his wife. But time had a way of forcing people into situations that they might not have thought of before and being separated for so long...Tate wasn't so sure Ava cared for him any more than as a friend.

"You must speak with her and see. Maybe she will surprise you and have room for you and your hefty title. Yes, you are a duke, a man with multiple estates and people depending on you, but Miss Knight was willing to be mistress of all that before your parents became involved. If she loves you, and there is always a chance that two people destined for each other can make their way back to be with one another, she will make room for you in her life as well."

Tate grinned at his friend. "You've become a romantic since meeting Rosa."

Scott laughed. "That, I have, and I'm proud of it too. But you'll see I'm right. If you're patient and as you once were with Miss Knight, there is no reason why she would not fall in love with you again."

If only that were so and he would hope for such a thing. Once he returned to Berkshire, slowly and with caution, he would try to ease his way back into her affections. It wouldn't be easy, even if they were on friendly terms once more. A lot could happen in five years, people changed and so did their goals and their dreams.

His certainly had. After idling his time in London over the past two years, rumor reached him that the thoroughbred Titan would be sent to Tattersalls for sale, and his disregarded dream of owning and running his own horse racing and breeding program burst back to life. He'd returned to Berkshire, even with the knowledge that Ava was only three miles from him, but he had wanted to fight for what he'd once imagined doing. Not being just a duke, but a man with interests, a profession that he not only enjoyed, but loved.

He drank down the last of his champagne. He would succeed in winning her, he would succeed in joining their estates and making all their dreams come to fruition. "You make excellent points, Lord Brandon."

"Well, if Miss Knight is your future, then yes, the past must be dealt with and moved on from. I'm happy for you and I wish you well with your lady. I remember how broken you were. You may disagree with me, and I can see from your face that you do," Scott said, chuckling. "But when you speak of this Miss Knight, you shine. She is a light for you, bright and true. I hope you're able to win back her love."

Tate smiled, clasping his friend on the shoulder. "Thank you. I shall take your good wishes and hope for the best as well. A lot has happened in the past five years, it may take some time for us to find our way back to each other, but I'm determined."

"I hope you do, and be sure to bring Miss Knight to my wedding if you're successful. Rosa would love to meet her, I'm sure."

"That my friend is something I shall promise you,"

Tate said, hoping that in turn he would soon be able to invite Lord Brandon to his wedding also.

~

*T*ate sat at the breakfast table the following morning, thankfully alone. The smell of hot brewing coffee permeated the air, the Times was freshly pressed and his breakfast of bacon, poached eggs and sliced ham sat before him. He leaned back in his chair, enjoying this quiet time, eating breakfast in solitude.

The door to the room opened and in bundled his mother. He folded his paper, sighing at his moment of peace would now be short-lived. "Good morning, Mother," he said, picking up his knife and fork.

His mother sat herself at the table, asking a nearby footman to serve her tea and her usual breakfast of toast and butter. "I did not know you were coming back to London, my dear. What has brought you to town, since I'm soon to join you at Cleremore."

"I had business in town." At his curt answer, she merely raised her brow and turned back to her meal.

Tate ate for a moment, thinking over all that he wanted to say to her. Fighting to remain calm and not lose his temper. "Did you enjoy your evening last night? How many balls would that make this year? Three?"

His mother threw him a sweet smile. "It was, in fact. How wonderful you're keeping tabs on my parties. And I'm glad you arrived in time for last night's entertainment, since you disappeared before the Season and have not returned these past ten months!"

"I think that is an exaggeration. I have been to town sporadically for different matters pertaining to the estates."

"Do not vex me, boy, for I am very annoyed. How can you leave London when so many eligible, wealthy women are here for the taking? All ready to dip a curtsy and marry a duke. Might I remind you of Lady Clapham who is more than eligible, a widow who seems to enjoy your company, or so I hear. But no, you run off to Berkshire and your silly horse hobby never to return. I despair of you."

Tate would've loved nothing more than to tell his dearest Mother that Berkshire too hailed some very sweet and perfectly acceptable women who could be his bride. Well, one in particular.

"I need to be in Berkshire as I've recently acquired one of England's most treasured racehorse. And if it has not missed your attention, you do remember me writing to you regarding the stables. You know," he said, gaining her attention, "the ones that burned down."

She waved his statement away. "I do remember you mentioning both those things, but I fail to see how this is so important enough to keep you from town." She paused, taking a sip of coffee. "How are the stables coming along?"

"They are being rebuilt as we speak, and they didn't simply burn down, as I said in my letter, I believe the fire was started deliberately. I have hired a Bow Street Runner to investigate, but be sure not to repeat that. I do not want anyone to know I harbor suspicions."

"Very well," she sighed, picking up a piece of toast. "I will not say a word."

"Good, which brings me to another matter for which I'm in town, and that concerns you."

His mother placed down her toast, complaining it was cold. A servant picked up the plate and took it away before his parent bothered to look in his direction. "Really. What is it you wanted of me?"

Tate placed down his cup of coffee. He wanted to see her face when he confronted her with this truth. "Why did you fabricate the letter that Miss Knight supposedly sent me all those years ago? Allowed me to believe that her affections were false, that she wished for a different way of life? That she did not want me?"

His mother's eyes went wide before her face paled to an awful shade of gray. In that moment, Tate knew without any doubt she had been behind the calculated way of separating them. He had hoped that possibly it was not true, but that did not seem the case.

"I don't know what you're talking about," she said fussing with a napkin. "Now let me eat my breakfast in peace. I have a busy day, many calls to make all afternoon."

He ground his teeth, better that than yell at his mother before all the staff. "You have plenty of time for your calls, I want to talk about your underhanded, cruel scheme."

His mother seemed to accept her defeat in this regard, lifted her chin, her lips pursed in a tight line. "Yes I wrote it and I would do it again. Your father and I thought it was best considering both your young ages. You had not even had your first Season and you were thinking of marrying a girl who had no rank, no nobility. A horse trainer's daughter, of all things." His mother shrill voice lifted at her last point and he cringed as pain coursed through his temples. "I spoke to Miss Knight's father and he was in agreement, after we explained how we would never countenance such a union and his daughter would be ruined by being cut by society."

He shook his head. His mother's cruelty had no bounds. So she'd even brought Mr. Knight into her scheme by threatening his only daughter's reputation. "Miss

Knight was more than a horse trainer's daughter to me. I never cared about rank, money, the title in the way you have. Miss Knight may have had humble beginnings, but she is equal to me in every way."

"Pfft," his mother spat. "She is not suitable for a duke's wife, nor will she ever be."

He took a calming breath. "You had no right to interfere in the way you did. Are you not ashamed to have played such a cruel trick on your son or the people who have been our neighbors for years now?"

"Mr. Knight, need I remind you, Tate, was also in agreement."

"You convinced the man he was, by threatening Ava."

"Do not tell me that you have offered for her hand yet again," she sneered. "I will never forgive you if you have."

"Not that it is any of your business, but no, I have not. At this time Miss Knight is no more than our neighbor and a woman who is housing all my horses after the fire. Even though there is no discussion of me and Ava being anything more than what we are now, it does not excuse what you did to us both. How could you do that to your own son? You knew how much I cared for her."

She shook her head, dismissing his words. "A childhood folly that would have ruined your life. You wish for me to be sorry at stopping such a union. Well," she paused, throwing her napkin on the table. "I will not and never shall."

"For years, you sent me away to a country that was not my own, all to keep me away from her. You could've been honest." Not that it would've changed his mind about Ava as his wife. Even now to the very core of Tate's soul, he knew that she was the right woman for him.

"My family treated you well in New York. They

lavished you with everything a young titled man of great wealth wanted at his feet. Women, parties, social events mingling with the best my country had to offer. Do not say to me that your life has been so unhappy and despondent when it has not. Do you think I did not hear the goings on about London regarding you, when you first returned? Of the many lovers, the gambling and so on. Do not be so quick to judge when I could've judged you two years ago upon your return."

How could she be so blind? Yes, he had enjoyed America, but that was only because he was forced to stay and could not leave. He had thought the woman he loved did not love him. "I will not forgive you for such duplicity."

"I suppose you're going to tell me that your interest in Berkshire these past months has nothing to do with Miss Knight being home from France. Please tell me that you've not taken up where you left off with that little nobody."

Tate fisted his hands on the table, his breakfast forgotten. "How dare you call her that? Do not *ever*," he said, making his mother start, "call her that again. Her name is Miss Ava Knight, and hear this, Mother. No matter what happens between me and Ava, know that I will not put up with your meddling. What I choose to do with my life or whom I select to be my bride is my choice. As head of the family if I wanted to marry a doxie from Soho I will." Tate stood, having had enough of this conversation.

"Do not threaten me. I'm still your mother and do not forget that I can make your life in Society easy or hard. Miss Knight hails from the lineage of servants. People who worked as our tenant farmers prior to purchasing a horse and racing it. Pure luck that it paid off for them and while I'm very happy they could drag themselves away from a life of servitude, that does not make her equal to the task of being a duchess."

He'd always thought his mother's light blue eyes pretty, but right at this moment they were cold and without an ounce of feeling.

"If you marry Miss Knight, make her the Duchess of Whitstone will be the laughing stock of the *ton*. I did not marry into nobility, sacrifice my life in my own country to live in England, just to watch my son marry a woman who would bring nothing but shame and a few mares to the marriage."

Tate clasped the table, leaning toward his mother. "Do not speak to me or about Ava in such a way again, mother. I'm warning you," he sneered. "I am the Duke of Whitstone and whomever I marry will be accepted by Society because if they do not, as a duke, they would rue the day they slighted her. That warning includes you too. If you wish to have anything to do with my future, you will not meddle in whom I choose as my bride."

His mother pushed back her chair. "There are many who are more suited as the future Duchess of Whitstone," she said, her voice shaking. "If you only gave them the opportunity, you would see that there are many who would be perfect for you. You must see that Miss Knight is not for you. She may satisfy some honor code that you think you're breaking by stepping away from the union, but it will not last forever. With people with backgrounds such as hers, there are always hidden skeletons that the *ton* is salivating to find out. It will be only a matter of time before her family and something that they have hidden in their past will come to light and ruin you. Ruin my future grandchildren's prospects."

"You talk rubbish."

"Do I?" she said. "Think of your male heir, away at Eton or Harrow. The bullying your children will suffer when they find out their mother bred horses. That the boy's grandparents were once tenant farmers. That, in itself, will be hard enough to bear, let alone some other scandal we do not know about yet."

He shook his head, not willing to listen any further. He strode to the door and then paused. "You're hysterical and I suggest you calm down. Heed my warning, Mother. I will banish you to the castle in Ireland if you do not obey and do as I want. You are no longer head of the family. Do not ever cross the line that will make me act upon my threat."

His mother glared at him, the little lace cap atop her head shaking with her temper.

"If you cared about the dukedom so very much, you would've come home when you heard about the fire. But instead, what do we find, merely more parties and balls for you to host. At least, Miss Knight cared enough to fight the fire alongside of me that night. Where were you, I wonder? Drinking champagne and enjoying the company you only believe are of value to you. It would not occur to you to think of others, but Miss Knight does and that is why she will always be suitable as my wife. There is not a selfish bone in her body."

"You have no idea what you're talking about or what you need. Just like your father. Easy to lead astray."

"I will be returning to Berkshire in a few days. I think it is best that once you've finished the little season that you re-locate yourself to one of the other properties other than Cleremore Hall."

"You would throw out your mother for a nobody?"

Tate glanced at his parent, disgusted by her words. "Because of your actions, of sending me away to America,

I missed saying goodbye to my father. You allowed me to blame an innocent woman for that instead. Miss Knight may be a nobody to you, but she is everything to me. And always has been. No matter how many years you took to try and change that fact, it will never change." He left her staring after him and headed for the door. After such a confrontation, Whites sounded perfect right about now. Anything would be better than here.

CHAPTER 8

*a*few days later Ava looked up from the chair she sat in on the terrace when she heard the sound of wheels on the gravel drive. She shaded her eyes against the sun low on the horizon, and shutting the book she was reading, she tried to make out who was paying her a visit.

As the carriage came into view on her drive, she stood and started for the front of the house, her curiosity getting the better of her. The black equipage was covered in dust from its many miles of travel, and there was a range of traveling chests atop the vehicle. Her heart leapt with joy and she started to run when she recognized the dark head of curls peeking out the carriage window.

She waved. "Hallie, is that you?" Ava laughed, beyond happy to see her friend. Hallie had been one of the first girls to have befriended her at school in France. Her no-nonsense manner and outspokenness had redeemed her in Ava's eyes and she loved that she was so bold, so opinionated. Not that looking at her you would guess such a thing. She was all delicate softness at a glance. Her dark locks, with a natural curl, were the envy of all their friends and her fierce green eyes echoed intelligence far beyond Ava's comprehension. Hallie was simply an English rose, but one who loved far harsher climes than any such plant could tolerate.

"Ava," Hallie shouted back before opening the door and jumping down without assistance. Her dearest friend ran and pulled her into a fierce hug, one which Ava reciprocated. She'd not seen her friend in a year, and to have her here and now and in Berkshire was a dream.

"Hallie," she said, hugging her tightly. "Oh, I'm so happy to see you." Tears pooled in her eyes and drawing back, she noted her friend's eyes were too a little watery.

"It has been too long, my dearest. How is England? How are your magnificent horses doing?" Hallie asked, looking over toward the stables.

"They're all doing fabulously well." At least the horses were doing well, as for her life, well, that was up for debate. "How was Egypt and all those magnificent Pharaohs you love so much?"

Hallie laughed, pulling off her hat and looking up at the sky. "They are perfect in every way. And one day you must come and visit me there. I know you'd love it so very much."

The idea of seeing such a hot, ancient and cultured land filled her with jealousy that she'd not traveled as far and wide as Hallie had. The woman was so intelligent and worldly, and had arrived at the most perfect time. "I cannot believe that you're here. How long are you staying?" Ava led her indoors, dragging her toward her parlor, and ordered tea and lunch to be served in there today instead of the dining room.

Hallie looked about the room, picking up some of the old antiquities that Ava's father had collected, studying a vase or curio, before sitting them back down. "For a month or so, if you'll have me. I have some business to attend to in London at the museum. The new benefactor there is refusing to accept a stone tablet we found on the Egyptian plateau to be authentic. I do believe it's because a woman found it, namely me." Hallie sat her hat on a nearby chair and slumped into the seat, sighing.

Ava sat also, smiling at her friend's carefree and easy manner. How she'd missed her. "Congratulations on finding such a magnificent piece of history. I'm sure you will persuade the gentleman that it is what you say." She couldn't wipe the smile from her lips at having her friend here. "I cannot tell you how happy this makes me that you've come to stay. Not because of the trouble you're having, but because I'll have a month of your company. It'll be like old times."

"Talking of which," Hallie said, glancing inquisitively her way. "I heard a funny little rumor in town before I started toward Berkshire. Do you want to know what it was?"

Ava leaned back onto the settee and kicked off her slippers, folded her legs up on the seat beneath her. Did she want to listen to idle, silly chatter that floated about London on a regular basis? No, not really, but her friend's demeanor, the naughty twinkle in her gaze made her curious. "Very well, what is London all in a flutter about?" she asked, already dreading her failing at being drawn into tattletales.

"You're the neighbor of the Duke of Whitstone, are you not?"

The mention of Tate had her sitting forward and a pang of fear shot through her not knowing where the conversation was headed. "I've know the duke for some years, yes." Ava had not told a soul of his slighting of her when she'd started school in France. Hallie had been one of her school friends, and seemed content not to pry into her past. All of them, the five friends she'd made, had their own secrets to keep hidden, she supposed. To be jilted was not something any young woman of any social stature wanted to be reminded of, so Ava had tried to push it away and carry on with her life the best she could.

Now that she knew that Tate had never rejected her, well, it changed things somehow, and she was desperate to talk to someone other than the man himself about it. Her life here at Knight Stables had become her whole world. Being away at school had taught her to trust and rely on herself and no one else and, over the years, she'd become independent. She had the ability to carry on with her life content and happy without the bounds of matrimonial bliss. Not that Tate was the only other reason she had shied away from marriage, her disastrous run-in with Lord Oakes had cemented within her the decision that being a woman of independent means was preferable to being at the whim of any husband.

"Rumor has it he's returned to town and has quit his mistress's home. The whole town is in uproar, or at least Willow is saying so. Some were shocked that he had one at all, since it was so very discreet, but alas, it's been revealed and this is what is being said."

Willow Perry was another school friend Ava had met in France and resided in London most of the year with her titled aunt. "What did Willow say?" Ava asked, having not known the duke had a permanent lover. Of course, the mistake was hers. He'd been famous for his dalliances, his socializing and gambling ways since his return from America. It was only natural he would have such a permanent fixture to sate his needs. She steeled herself to listen, her stomach churning at the thought of him with another woman.

"Only that she is free to do as she pleases, even though some say there was never an agreement of exclusivity in the first place. That it was simply a mutually satisfying union and nothing else."

Ava swallowed the bile that rose in her throat. "Oh, well," was all she could manage.

Hallie continued. "When he returned from America two years ago, people stated that the moment he'd seen her at her husband's funeral no less, the mutual attraction was undeniable."

"She was married?"

"Oh yes," Hallie went on. "She's a titled lady. Lady Clapham, a Viscountess from all accounts."

Ava was lost for words. Tate's lover was a lady of his own class. Her mind whirred at the thought of it. Why had he not offered for her hand? Why end it now after so long...

"The *ton* is full of questions as to what has occurred between them and without most of them ever knowing. When I heard that he was your neighbor, well, I simply had to ask." Hallie smiled, thankfully completely unaware her news threatened to tear Ava's heart out of her chest.

"I had not heard. Just because we're neighbors does not mean that I have anything to do with his personal life. He may do whatever he pleases, as I shall."

Ava looked away, staring at nothing in particular. Her stomach churned at the idea of Tate sleeping with another woman. Up until this, point she'd purposefully not imagined such a horror of him marrying or loving someone else. The duke was his own man. Responsible for his own actions and could do whatever he liked.

"Of course, my dear." Hallie studied her a moment. "Did you know the duke when he was a young man? Gossip says he is one of the most handsome men in England. Is it true? It's has been so long since I've been in this country, I no longer know a soul, other than you and our friends from school, of course. You'll have to enlighten me on all of this, Ava."

"Well, I hate to disappoint you, Hallie, but your little tidbit of gossip is the first thing I've heard in months from town. I've been so busy with the horses and getting the estate up and running, keeping the racehorses fit and healthy that I don't have time to socialize." And it was how it ought to be. Ava couldn't think of a more delightful way to spend her time than outdoors, riding horses or grooming them. Being a successful woman in a man's business. "I find myself very content with this sort of life."

"Really?" Hallie asked, scrutinizing her for a moment. "Are you really content? None of us are getting any younger and most of the girls we went to finishing school with are married with children. I had thought you wished for such a future." Her friend settled back in her chair, crossing her legs. "I must admit, as much as I love being an historian, traveling to foreign lands, I do wonder what my life might have been like had I returned to England after completing our studies and married. My parents, God rest their souls, would've loved nothing more, and I feel I let them down a little bit by following my own path."

Ava, too, had let her father down. Before his death she had known he'd longed for grandchildren to see them grow up and eventually inherit his racing dynasty. For a time she'd thought to give him his wish, a path that had almost brought on her ruin. After that, Ava had been determined to ignore Society norms and expectations, had let it be known that Miss Ava Knight of Knight Stables was in no way looking for a husband.

Even so, with all her independence, and guarding of that status, one man still had the ability to haunt her dreams when she slept at night. *Tate.*

Ava stood and strode over to the mantle and rang to find out what had happened to delay luncheon. She moved over to the window pulling back the blue and cream velvet curtain to look out onto the lawns. "You will get an opportunity to meet the Duke of Whitstone. He is staying here at present. His stables, you see, where destroyed in a fire and all his horses are being stabled here until his own are rebuilt. I'm sure once he returns from London you, will meet. Maybe by then there will be a new rumor about his grace, and his proclaiming of a new lover."

Hallie chuckled. "You do not fool me, Miss Ava Knight. When I mentioned the duke and that he was removing Lady Clapham from his life, I did not fail to see that your face fell at the realization he had a lover. You say you knew the duke for many years, but I wonder how well did you know him? Because to me, I cannot help but think that you knew him very well indeed."

Ava refused to glance in her friend's direction. Hallie had always been so good at reading people. It was a trait they'd used often at school, have Hallie determine the mood of their teachers so they'd know if they could be a little naughty or needed to be nice. Now, in her parlor, her friend's insight was not welcome.

"Knowing that he had a lover has hurt you and I'm sorry, Ava."

She sighed, not wanting to lie to her friend anymore. For years she'd kept the pain hidden, but there was no more reason to do so. Hallie was her friend and she should've confided in her years ago. "To hear such news is shocking, I'll admit, but nothing that isn't happening all the time within the *ton*," she admitted quietly. A little part of her still dreamed of them, longed to go back and fight for what she'd wanted five years ago. But as much as it hurt to have lost him, through no fault of their own, Ava had come to realize that it was for the best.

She was not made to be a duchess. To attend balls and parties, to be a hostess of the highest caliber of the *ton*. Such a life simply wasn't for her. So, in a way, their parents had done them a favor by lying and separating them. For there was no doubt in Ava's mind that she would've failed at being a duke's wife and eventually Tate would've become frustrated and disappointed in her lack of social graces. She could never have borne his disappointment. And no duchess should be anything but proper, undamaged, perfect in every way, and she was none of those things.

"I've never met a duke before," Hallie said, changing the subject. "Will I like him, do you think?" she asked, smiling a little.

"I think you will," Ava answered, nibbling her lip as she thought about Tate. "He is nice enough and is pleasant to all his staff." A knock on the door sounded and bidding them enter, a servant carrying a silver tray of tea, cold meats and bread into the room. He placed it on the wooden table before the settee before bowing and leaving them alone.

Ava busied herself pouring the tea, placing one spoon of sugar into Hallie's cup, as she remembered she liked it, with a dash of milk, and she held it out to her friend. Hallie took the tea and met Ava's gaze over the cup's rim. "Why do I get the impression that you're not telling me something? Does the duke's parting from Lady Clapham have anything to do with you, Ava?"

Ava shut her mouth with a snap. She sat, hoping that the heat proceeding up her neck wasn't noticeable to her friend. "How should I know what the duke's thoughts are on his mistress?" Ava said, sipping her tea.

"I think you know a great deal more than you're saying," Hallie grinned mischievously.

She sighed, running one finger along the side of the porcelain saucer her tea cup sat on. "The duke is here merely because of the circumstances that have happened at his estate. An unfortunate circumstance that was very dangerous. He's hired a Bow Street Runner, you know. When they looked into the fire at his Cleremore Hall they found that it was possibly started on purpose. That someone actually wanted to hurt innocent horses, of all things."

Hallie frowned at Ava's words, all mirth gone. "Although I do not enjoy riding the animals myself, to think that someone would try and injure so many horses must be terribly upsetting. Please tell me that all of his cattle survived."

"Yes, thankfully," Ava said. "We were able to get them all out in time, but his two stables were unsalvageable." She thought back on the night, when they had collapsed onto the ground after exiting the stable that burned behind them. She could still smell her singed hair, the pain that occurred with each breath. Seeing Tate lying beside her, gasping for breath was a sight she never wished to see again. The crippling fear that he could've died had been telling, and she'd known in that moment that she still cared for him. When Tate had reached up and wiped the dusting of soot from her cheek, even now her heart fluttered in her chest.

"And so now, he's here to stay," Hallie grinned once more and Ava fought not to roll her eyes. "And you are friends. I am not ashamed to say as your friend also, that I would love to see you make such a grand match. Do you think you'll ever marry?" Hallie asked."

"Not now," Ava said quickly. "I think that time has passed for such an event, and I am well on the shelf. I'm four and twenty do not forget."

Hallie narrowed her fierce, green eyes. "What about taking a lover? You would not be the first woman to do so, or the last."

Ava shuddered at the thought. The idea bringing back memories she'd rather forget. "No, I would not like that."

Hallie sighed, sitting back on her chair and resting her head against its back. "I had one, you know, in Egypt. He was a Major General or Liwa' as they term them. He was deadly handsome just as his sword skills were, but it wasn't enough to save him. They went on patrol just outside of Cairo, a small skirmish in an outlying village, and he was killed by locals."

Hallie was quiet a moment and Ava didn't know what to do, having no idea her friend had been in love. "His skin was so dark and beautiful, like copper under an Egyptian sky. His dark hair and features even now make my heart beat fast. He had the longest eye lashes I've ever seen or ever will see on a man, I'm sure."

Hallie met her gaze, her eyes overly bright. "It was one of the reasons why I have returned home to England. Everywhere I looked in Cairo I saw him, had memories of our times together." Hallie shook her head, sighing. "It was too hard to stay."

Ava stood and went to sit beside her friend, pulling her into a tight embrace. Having had no idea her friend had been through so much. So many secrets between them all. "Dearest Hallie, I'm so sorry for your loss. If you gave your heart to him he must've been a good, honorable man. I'm glad that you came home and you are more than welcome to stay here as long as you need to heal your heart."

"Thank you, Ava. I knew you would understand. You know that I no longer have any family, that I'm an orphan in fact, and so I need my friendships at this time."

"I wish I could've met him," Ava said, wiping a tear from her friend's cheek.

Hallie sniffed and Ava reached into her pocket and took out her handkerchief, handing it to her friend. "I do not know how it happened exactly, only that some of his men returned bloody and almost dead themselves. Omar never returned and some days later, more soldiers went out to find him and found him where he'd fallen. They buried him and that was all the closure I received."

"Oh, Hallie." Ava rubbed her back, trying to give comfort where there was no comfort to be given for such a thing. To lose one's love was not a severing that one could get over easily. Ava knew this as well as anyone, for it had taken her years to get over Tate and his abandoning of her, if she ever did. "Tell me what I can do, Hallie, to make it better for you." How could she not see under her friend's laughter and good humor that she'd been suffering from a personal loss? She cursed her own feeble troubles that paled in comparison and her blindness to them.

"Just being here with you is good enough for me and I will get over my pain eventually, I'm sure. But I shall never forget him, he was the loveliest man, even if our backgrounds and religions were so very different."

Ava hugged her again. "If you gave your heart to him, I have absolutely no doubt that he was a wonderful person. As you are and only such people have amazing things happen to them."

Hallie smiled through her tears and Ava promised she would be here for her friend for as long as she needed her.

"Now that you know my sad little story," Hallie said, reaching to pour more tea, "will you tell me the truth of yours."

Ava gave a self-deprecating laugh. How intelligent Hallie was to see through her words and demand the truth that lay behind them. She shook her head in awe of her wiles. "Very well, since we are both telling each other the truth of our lives, our sad pasts, I will tell you the truth of mine.

She settled back on the settee, folding her hands in her lap. "Five years ago, the duke, who was a marquess then, and myself thought ourselves in love. Looking back at the time now, I have no doubt that I did love him, wildly in fact. We were willing to run away and marry. It has only come to light recently that our parents put a stop to that plan that neither one of us knew about. We were dispatched oceans apart. I, for France, and the school that I came to know you at. The duke to America to his mother's family. We believed each other indifferent. We believed that the other had broken trust. This is not the case and now that we know the truth, well…"

Ava stood and started to pace, the percale cotton of her gown swooshing with each determined step. She stopped at the mantel, holding onto the polished marble and hating the fact that they had been deceived so. Lied to by the people they loved and trusted above all else.

"Now, I don't know where we're at. I don't know what I feel anymore. I love my life. I love the horses and the races. I can ride astride and I can gallop across the fields whenever I wish. I don't have to go to town and I don't have to take part in the Season. I'm not at the beck and call or an ornament to a husband's whim. I like this way of life, to be my own master."

Understanding dawned at how difficult her life had become with Tate's return. How messy it was all of a sudden. When did that happen? A month ago she hadn't had any of these concerns, now it was all she thought about. Could she give up her life here and become a duchess? Would that be something Tate would expect of her? Ava bit her lip, not sure now that she'd tasted freedom that she could ever become someone else's property again. That Tate did not know her as well as he once had, when he found out the truth, even if she wished to be his wife, he might find her lacking.

Hallie picked up her tea and took a sip. "Do you think that the duke still likes you in that way? You are friends, you said, could you wish for more and still enjoy this life here in the country? Even as a duchess?"

Ava didn't think this life would be possible if she became Tate's wife. A duke was one of the highest of the peerage. Society loved nothing more than to have them at their parties and events. Tate would want her by his side in town every Season, and she would be a nobody, new money perhaps but little else. A woman who had married above her station. Talked to yes, and then talked about behind closed doors.

"I confess that I do still think of him when I'm alone. I think about what it would be like to be taken into his arms once more. Trapped against his hard chest where I might run my hands up over the corded muscles that I know lie beneath his clothing." To have the touch of his lips against hers, to have him make her his haunted her dreams. Ava opened her eyes and turned back to her friend. "I don't know what's wrong with me. I thought myself past all this silly infatuation."

"I think," Hallie said, leaning over and buttering a scone before placing it on a small plate. "That you still like the duke and that maybe you need to find out if he likes you as well."

Ava sighed seeing the logic behind her friend's plan, but the nerves that pooled in her belly at the thought of being so bold would make the fruition of it hard to complete. "That is the problem. I know I like him. But it is not what I thought my life would be like and I'm not sure I want him enough to give up everything that I have now. I would have to give up this life if I were to become a duchess. And can you really see me at balls and parties, dressed up in silks and chiffons, wearing the height of fashion and jewels. That is not who I am."

"I think you would make a wonderful duchess," Hallie said with some gumption. "Even so, it sounds to me that you have a lot of thinking to do. And you do not need to make any decisions now. I'm assuming the duke's stables are being rebuilt and he will return home very soon."

"Yes the stables are coming along very well. In fact, if

you want, I could show you tomorrow. We could ride down to the Hall and look them over. It will fill in a little of our time, at least."

Hallie smiled. "That sounds simply perfect."

Ava, content for now to talk about other things, pushed her musings about the duke out of her mind. She would dwell on him when she was alone. "You must tell me what you would like to have for dinner. What is your favorite meal? I'll have cook prepare it for you."

Hallie leaned back in her chair, seemingly a woman without a care in the world. How very wrong everyone would be to make that assumption.

"I would simply delight in having anything that is not a goat or sheep. I don't think I could stomach another bowl of rice either."

"Consider it done," Ava said. "And I will go and organize this now and confirm that your room is ready for you too. I'm sure you're very tired after your travels today."

"Thank you, Ava." Hallie leaned over and taking her hand, squeezed it a little. "I'm so thankful that we are friends."

Ava laid her hand over Hallie's. "As am I, dearest. As heartbroken as I was, my traveling to France for school was worth it, in the end. You, Evie, Willow, and Molly made it all better again and I am so glad that it was so."

～

The following day Ava and Hallie made their way to the duke's estate. The sound of hammering and sawing of wood, the gentle hum of male chatter as they worked carried toward them. They stopped atop the small hill that overlooked the estate, watching for a moment and allowing the horses to catch their breath. A highly polished black carriage sat before the front of the estate. Footmen swiftly carried in a siege of traveling trunks.

"Do you think the duke's back?" Hallie asked, casting a glance in Ava's direction.

Ava took in the details of the horse that was being led toward a nearby holding yard. "I think he may be, but I do not think he is alone. Dread pooled in Ava's stomach with the unfortunate thought that his mother had returned with him from town. The woman was the only surviving parent who separated her and the duke all those years ago, and Ava was not the forgiving type. Not for such things as decisions borne out of spite and social pressure.

They walked on, halting not far from where the new stables were being built. A nearby builder tipped his cap at them, greeting them warmly. He spoke to them for a short time, detailing the progress and explained how the new design would differ from the old. It looked marvelous. The new building of red brick construction, and almost all the walls were completed, while some men were on the roof fixing the tiled shingles. The smell of freshly cut pine permeated the air.

"It is coming along well," the duke said, walking out of the stable and greeting them with a smile. "Do you not agree?"

Ava glanced down from atop her horse, taking in his Hessian boots and the tan breeches that highlighted his form for their visual pleasure. His hair, again, was mussed from travel, but otherwise his bright gaze was warm and inviting. Ava smiled, thrilled to see him again. She bit back a sigh. If she were to remain indifferent, merely friends, she would have to curb her appreciation of his handsomeness.

The week that he'd been gone had dimmed her memory of how very attractive he was. How the sight of him made her long for things, which she had not desired for five years. How was she ever going to continue on with her life as an independent, strong woman who did not need a husband to make her life complete when men like the duke walked about Berkshire?

The clearing of one's throat reminded Ava of her manners and she gestured toward her friend Hallie who threw amused glances at them both.

"Forgive me, Your Grace, this is my best friend Miss Hallie Evans. She's newly returned from Egypt. She's a historian."

The duke bowed. "It's a pleasure to meet you Miss Evans. Any friend of Miss Knight's is a friend of mine."

"Thank you, Your Grace, how very kind of you." Again Hallie threw her an amused, knowing smile before sliding down off her horse.

Ava did also, and handing the horses off to a waiting stable boy, started toward the main house.

"I was about to have tea." Tate caught Ava's gaze and, for the life of her, she could not look away. Much to her annoyance she would have to admit to having missed him the past week. Even knowing that he'd been in town, meeting with friends and one of which was Lady Clapham, did not lessen that feeling. Was she possibly the reason he'd broken with his lover?

"We would not like to intrude. I wanted to show Hallie the stables, and did not expect to find you home," Ava said, slowing her steps.

"Thank you for the invitation, Your Grace," Hallie

replied, clasping Ava's arm and pulling her toward the house. "I, for one, would love a cup of tea."

"If you have somewhere else that you wish to be, that is fine also," Tate said, no doubt sensing Ava's reluctance.

"We have nowhere else to be," Hallie answered before Ava could get a word in. "I see the carriage is being unloaded with a great deal of luggage. Do you bring company back from town to Berkshire?"

The duke cleared his throat. "Ah, no I have not, but it would seem my mother has returned to stay for a time. I had thought she was traveling to one of my other estates that's located in Surrey, but I find her here..."

The thought that it was indeed his parent left a sour taste in Ava's mouth and for a moment, it was almost impossible to look pleased and polite for him that his Mother was back in Berkshire. The woman was a viper, and now knowing she'd separated them via lies and deceit... well, she would be lucky if Ava ever changed her opinion of the woman.

They continued toward the house before Tate turned to her, catching her gaze. "My mother's arrival will mean that my stay at Knight Stables will have to come to an end. But be assured I'll leave my best stableman at your disposal and my staff will continue to train my horses, and keep vigilance to ensure that what happened here does not occur at your own estate."

Ava was thankful for his help, but knowing that he would no longer be so close to her sent a pang of melancholy to swamp her. Over the month that he had been at her estate she'd grown used to seeing him about. Working the horses, wearing buckskin breeches and shirt and nothing else. The lovely, delightful glimpses of him had been were pleasing indeed.

With the lack of cravat and his shirt often out of his breeches, he could've passed as any one of her stable staff. Except for the fact that he held himself with years of ducal breeding behind him, the perfect straight aristocratic back and broad shoulders and thin waist. The intelligent mind that was always working behind gray eyes, made him stand out from anyone else.

Had always made him stand out...

A woman came to stand outside the front door, and the scowl on the dowager duchess' face told Ava all she needed to know. If she'd silently prayed that Tate's mother had mellowed over the years, the hope was eliminated in an instant, along with any hope that she felt even the tiniest fraction of remorse in separating her son from the woman he'd loved.

"Perhaps it is better that we return home, Your Grace," Ava said quickly. "You and the dowager duchess have traveled quite a way today and we don't want to intrude."

"Do not go." His words were softly spoken, so much so that Hallie continued on unaware of his whispered plea.

"I think it is best. Your mother does not look pleased to see me again."

Tate took in his mother's appearance before turning back to Ava. "I never had you down for a woman who cared for what others thought."

If he was baiting her into going inside...well, it was working. If there was one thing Ava disliked above anything else, that was being beaten by a foe. And the dowager Duchess of Whitstone was certainly that.

~

*U*shering everyone indoors and toward the back parlor that captured the warm afternoon sun, Tate ordered tea and refreshments and reveled in the fact that he was home. It had only been a week and yet to be back in Berkshire, his main country seat, and only a few short miles from Ava was a pleasure indeed.

He'd missed her while away in town, and having seen her inspecting his stables today along with her friend, had brought a burst of joy unlike any he'd known for many years. He supposed it was somewhat similar to what he'd felt upon stepping foot on English soil after his years away in America.

His decision to remove Lady Clapham from his life had been a decision he was well pleased with too. He hoped, in the weeks to come, he could prove to Ava once more that she would be perfect as his wife and future Duchess of Whitstone. As independent as she had become, to have her beside him in town, to be his duchess, to have her caring, thoughtful, guiding hand within his life was what he wanted most. He'd idled away his time for so long, in a way lost without her. Being a duchess did come with responsibilities, but he was certain Ava was up to those obligations.

They sat before the bank of windows overlooking the outdoors. The silk floral pattern on the settee and other furniture suited the feminine feel of the room and its location overlooking a rose garden.

Choosing to stand, Tate waited for his mother to initiate conversation with their guests, but at her continued silence, her steely gaze as they waited for tea, he stepped in and introduced Ava once more, along with Miss Evans.

"Miss Evans has recently returned from Egypt, Mother," Tate said, trying to dispel the tension in the room.

His mother's expression remained unimpressed. "Egypt, you say, pray explain what a young woman such as yourself is doing in such a remote and harsh environment. Quite an odd location for you, one would think."

Hallie smiled all sweetness and yet the look in her eyes told Ava that her friend was not fooled by the dowager and her calculating ways. "I have been in Egypt for the last two years studying tombs, pyramids and some locations along the Nile. I suppose you could say I have been digging in the sand and trying to find ancient graves and artifacts. Although that is probably too simple an explanation for what I do."

"And you intend to return? Do you not wish to marry?" The dowager looked over Hallie with a studied air. "You are quite on the shelf, if I may say so, Miss Evans."

Tate had to give Miss Evans points for not outwardly showing offence to his mother's comments. He threw his mother a warning glance which she turned her nose up at and ignored.

"I'm in England for only a short time, to see my friends, Ava included, and to finish some business in London. But I shall return to Egypt or some other place that offers such a rich historical locale, you can be sure."

"Are you staying long in Berkshire, Your Grace?" Ava asked, smiling a little at his mother and gaining nothing but a cold, calculating stare back.

"I will be staying here for some weeks. There are some friends that I would like to catch up with in the county and, of course, my son."

Tate didn't believe that for a moment and he didn't bother to mention to his parent that they had seen each other only this week in town. Or that she wasn't supposed to be here but at the dower house.

"I was telling Miss Knight and Miss Evans that the stables will be ready soon. It'll mean my horse stock will not have to impinge on your time any longer, Miss Knight." Not that he wanted to bring them back. With his horses at Ava's home, it gave him the opportunity to see her often, to talk and have privacy.

"That is good news, darling," his mother said. "A duke should be at his estate if he's not in town attending to his many duties there."

Hallie gasped and turned it into a cough. Tate sighed at his mother's thinly veiled insult.

"Miss Knight, I can tell you now that I'm back from London, I'm more than happy to allow Titan cover your mare. As soon as she is in heat, we shall try them together."

His mother mumbled something under her breath, but Ava beamed at him. "You will? Oh, thank you, Your Grace. I'm very happy you've changed your mind."

He smiled at her and could see she wanted to hug him, a trait she'd often partaken in when they were younger and she was excited about something she cared for. He had missed her pretty face and beautiful soul. Her fine features were without fault, her skin like alabaster, except for her nose where a skimming of freckles ran across her cheeks. Her eyes sparkled with excitement, her dark lashes and perfectly arched brows would be the envy of town when she arrived on his arm. How his mother could think her common was beyond him. She was far superior to him in every way that mattered.

"Do we really need to discuss such things, Tate, my dear? The conversation is not really appropriate, don't you think?" His mother said, her tone full of censure and aimed at Ava.

"What would you prefer we talk about, Mother? The latest town gossip, or what scandals are going about your set? Neither of which interest me."

"They interest me and that's all that matters, is it not?" The dowager smirked. "I did hear some gossip about a certain gentleman of the peerage who was being foolish and willing to bring scandal upon his family. Now," she said, tapping her finger against her chin. "Let me think while I try and remember who it was about."

Tate glared at his mother who was walking a very fine line.

He turned his attention back to Ava. "Talking of my prized stallion, how is Titan, Miss Knight? I hope he's been behaving himself at your stables, not prancing around too much in front of the mares?" The horse as fast and brilliant as he was, was also vain, if horses could have such a trait.

"All your horses are in the best of health, and some of your grooms have had them out on the gallop this morning doing some time trails. I think you'll be pleased with how some of your yearlings are coming along."

What a marvelous woman she was, intelligent and passionate. She had a love for the same activities as he. In fact, it was Ava's father who'd sparked Tate's passion for racing, and he really owed the direction of his life outside of the ducal holdings to her father.

"You still enjoy running about and mucking out stables, Miss Knight. I see the finishing school in France has not cured you of that." His mother bore a self-satisfied smile and without an ounce of remorse at her inappropriate words, met Ava's gaze.

Tate glared at his mother. "There is more——"

"I find, Your Grace," Ava said, interrupting him, "that you are right. Finishing school did not cure me of my passions, any of them, and now that I'm back in Berkshire I'm well pleased with what's before me." Ava threw Tate a look of pure devilment, and unable to stop himself he chuckled. His mother's mouth puckered into a line of displeasure.

"I suppose we should hire your services, Miss Knight, and have you work in our stables since you're so fond of such pastimes. What does a stable hand earn these days, Tate dear?" his mother asked him, her voice dripping with innocent sweetness.

"Miss Knight is a successful businesswoman, Mother. She does not seek employment here." Tate threw his parent a warning glance, at which she tipped her nose up and ignored. If he had to, he would escort her out of the room before she insulted Ava anymore.

Without missing a beat, Ava said, "You know as well as I, Your Grace, that I inherited my family's business, property and land. In fact, if I wanted, I could waltz about London and take part in the very same events as you, so unfortunately in this case, you're unable to afford what it would cost you to have me work here."

The dowager narrowed her eyes. "You are wrong, Miss Knight. The spheres in which I circulate do not have young women from trade among their set. Which surprises me as to why I'm having to host you here at all for tea."

"Well' I suppose' that's because your son the duke invited us, not you. So technically you're not hosting us anything," Ava said, taking a sip of her tea as if the conversation were about the weather.

There was a light knock at the door and a footman

came in carrying tea and pastries before any more words could be spoken.

Tate had heard enough though, and walking over to his mother, he took her hand and pulled her to stand. "Please excuse us a moment," he said.

His mother smiled, but did not say another word as he towed her out of the room. Once safely out in the hall near the stairs, he rounded on her. "What has come over you? How could you be so rude? I warned you in London about such behavior. I will not stand for it."

His mother's face mottled in anger, her eyes flashing ire. "Do not bring that woman here again. She is not welcome and it's not fit for the likes of us, a Duke and a Duchess, to have to sit and have tea with a horse trainer."

Tate fought to rein in his fury. He took a step closer, pointing a finger at her upturned nose. "I will not have you speak to anyone that I invite into my home in such a way. You have a choice, Mother. Either go back into the parlor, apologize to Ava and be civil, or you can leave this estate."

His mother gasped. "You would oust your own Mother? The woman who gave birth to you for some servant who threw herself at your head before you were old enough to understand the implications of your foolish, youthful actions."

Tate ground his teeth, having heard enough. "Instruct your maid to repack your bags, if she's even finished unpacking them. You're leaving first thing tomorrow for London."

His mother stormed up the stairs. "I will not be going anywhere, Tate, and do not force my hand or I'll never forgive you."

Tate took a moment to regain his composure before re-entering the parlor, only to find it empty. He went back out into the hall, and opened the front door and in the distance, up near the stables he could see Ava and her friend getting back upon their mounts.

"Damn it," he swore, watching them a moment before closing the door. This was not how he wanted his time with Ava to end today after being away a week. His mother's presence here was going to make his time with Ava difficult and he would have to be on guard when she was present. For if one thing was for certain, his mother was up to no good and was hell bent, it would seem, in keeping them apart with any means possible, even blatant rudeness.

CHAPTER 9

I trusted in your love, your words and still I cannot understand how I could have been so wrong. That all that time you were trapped in an understanding you did not want. I'm sorry that you felt you could not be honest with me.

– An Excerpt from a letter from Miss Ava Knight to the Duke of Whitstone

Ava pushed Gallant Girl as fast as she could go down the gallop they trained the horses on. Today they were testing to see if the horse would make good time in a sprint and with any luck, win a few races leading up to Ascot.

"Great work," her head trainer said as she slowed the horse into a canter and eventually a trot. The horse's breathing was rapid, and in the crisp morning air, steam rose from both her body and out her nostrils.

Ava's heart gave a little flip when she spied Tate

standing beside her manager. He was taller than those about him, and today he was dressed in a large great coat with a gray fox fur collar snuggled close about his neck and keeping him warm. His wool cap finished off his casual look, and yet each time she saw him, he drew her in, tempted her like no one ever had before. Tempted her away from the life she had worked so hard to secure herself within.

She checked her face for any mud from the few horses that had been riding ahead of her and hoping she didn't look a sight, smiled. "What a pleasant surprise, Your Grace. I did not expect to see you here this early in the morning." She gave the horse one last rub and pat on her neck before sliding off. A young groom came over and took the horse's reins from her, before leading Gallant Girl back toward the stables where she'd get a well-earned rubdown.

"I was up early," the duke replied. "A little issue with the stables back home and thought to come and oversee my horses since they're still stabled here."

Ava had hoped he'd wanted to see her, but she nodded glad to see him no matter what reason. "Very good then, Your Grace."

Greg held up his pocket watch, smiling. "Good run today, Miss Ava. We may have a chance yet."

"Chance?" the duke asked, looking between them.

"We want to run Gallant Girl in Ascot next year. We think she has a chance of placing and she's never been more fit."

"Nothing ventured, nothing gained," Greg said, tipping his hat. "I'll be off then. I shall see you later, Miss Ava."

Ava nodded and turned her attention back to Tate who stood watching her. His intense inspection of her left her breathless and she hoped he did not notice the heat infusing her face right at this moment.

"If you have Gallant Girl racing at Ascot we may be up against each other." His deep voice made it hard to concentrate on what he was saying.

Ava pulled herself together and focused. "I have no hopes of winning, certainly not up against Titan, but I do hope to place. I think my Gallant Girl is capable of that."

"I would never doubt it." He gestured them to walk toward the house. "Can I escort you back to the house? There is something that I wish to discuss with you."

Ava studied him a moment and noticed his brow was furrowed. "Is there something the matter, Your Grace?" she asked.

He frowned, his mouth downcast. She didn't like seeing him so and she had an overwhelming urge to comfort him. A reaction she'd not had these past five years, not for anyone. "There has been another fire. This time it was at Lord and Lady Morton's estate in south Berkshire. The blaze started in the middle of the night, and sadly they've lost two horses and a stable lad." Tate rubbed a hand over his jaw and Ava realized he'd not shaved this morning.

"Oh dear God, no." Ava blinked back tears for the young stable boy's life which had been cut short and that of the poor horses. "How are Lord and Lady Morton?"

"Devastated, I would presume. I'm heading over there now and I wanted to know if you would like to come with me. Lady Morton may need a friend at this time, and I know she's very fond of you."

Ava was very fond of both Lord and Lady Morton in return. Lady Morton in particular had helped her through her troubles only last year, a support during a time that she'd prefer to forget. A cold shiver ran down her spine and she pushed the alarming memories away.

They were an elderly couple, and reminded Ava often of her own father who'd loved horses and country life and who hadn't been looking for anything grander than what was outside his front door. Her ladyship had been only too happy to give up Society and settle in the country and Ava had always loved that about them. They had done what made them happy and forgot what everyone else thought of the fact. A dream she and the duke once held themselves, but now with his many responsibilities away from Berkshire, she wasn't so sure he could leave London for months on end and bury himself in the country.

"Of course I'll come with you." Ava called out for her mare, Manny and within minutes they were cantering over the fields heading south toward the Mortons' estate.

With dew still on the ground and the birds tweeting their morning song, the sun rose to the side of them, warming the land and bringing forth a new day. Ava couldn't help but think of the terrible tragedy that the Morton's and the young stable lad's family would be going through right at this time.

"Do you think this fire has been started deliberately as well, Your Grace?"

Tate, riding beside her glanced her way and his look of contempt told her without words that he believed so. "The missive I received from Lord Morton stated a worker had witnessed a dark figure running from the stable where the first fire took hold. The worker raised the alarm straight away, and yet the stables took hold very quickly and it was out of hand before much could be done."

"You'll inform the Runner about this new incident."

Tate nodded. "I've sent my letter along with Lord

Morton's for evidence about the fire. I'm sure the Runner will be in Berkshire in the coming days. I've asked him to stay, incognito of course, and see what he can find out."

"I think that is best," she said. They rode for half an hour, the entire trip should not take them any longer than an hour in total. Tate slowed his mount as they came to a copse of trees and Ava followed suit. Her mind had been a whir of thoughts over the fires that were oddly circling her own estate. There was one other neighbor close by and she would send a note around to them to be on guard. Better to be safe than sorry.

"We shall rest the horses for a few minutes and continue on."

Ava pulled up beside him, and giving Manny some rein, allowed her to nibble on the grass at her feet. She took the opportunity to look around their surroundings. A flash of movement in the valley beyond caught her attention and she narrowed her eyes trying to see what it was that had moved.

"What is that over there in the trees?" She pointed toward where she'd seen the movement last and Tate followed suit. "Is that a man riding a horse along the base of the meadow?"

The person riding unawares that Ava and Tate were watching, came out of a wooded area and she caught sight of him. He was dressed in dark clothing, a long great coat and hat that was pulled low over his face, covering his features. He was headed north and seemed to be coming from a southerly direction. Odd, considering a man who was similarly dressed had just burned down the stables south of here...

"We should ride down and see who it is. Considering there has been a fire only hours ago, and now we see this gentleman riding north, it would only be right to question him. He may have seen someone or something," the duke said, continuing to watch.

Or he could be the culprit. Ava didn't say the words aloud, but she couldn't help but wonder. There was somebody in the area that was starting these fires. It could be anyone of their acquaintance or a stranger. At this point in time they could not exclude a soul.

Tate picked up his reins and kicked his mount forward. Ava did the same and they cantered toward the man, all the while the rider heading north had not noticed them. As they neared, the low thud of hooves on the damp sod beneath them made the gentleman aware of their presence.

He looked up, clearly surprised, and Ava pulled up her horse when she noticed he had a scarf tied about his face, covering his mouth and nose. Only his eyes were visible, but at this distance she still would never have been able to make out who it might be, if they knew him at all.

Without hesitation the man kicked his mount hard, and pushed the horse into a hard gallop. That his intention was to flee made the hair on the back of her neck rise, and Tate took chase, urging his horse in the direction the rider had gone.

They raced after him. The rider continued to push hard to get away from them, and Ava followed Tate over a small hedgerow, weaving their way through trees and across fields that didn't seem to slow the questionable man in the least.

The rider looked over his shoulder, and Ava heard him curse. Knowing Berkshire as well as she did, Ava realized they were coming to a part of the area that had a stream running through up ahead, some parts of it deep enough to swim in while others were shallow.

"He'll have to slow to pass the stream," she shouted out to Tate, pointing to the waterway that was now coming into view.

Tate nodded. "We'll get him there and find out what he's about."

Coming out of a small wooded area, a tree branch flicked back and hit Ava in the cheek, bringing tears to her eyes. She swiped at the sting, bringing her gloves away to see a little blood on them.

They followed him to the stream, and when Ava thought the man would halt and answer for his flight, he merely pushed his horse into the water to wade through. The horse's footing slipped and the man grappled for a moment, trying to keep his seat.

"Halt," Tate yelled, which the rider ignored, coming to the other side of the stream. "Why are you running?"

The man didn't bother to answer them, merely headed up a small hill. They lost sight of him a moment before Ava, studying the trees, found him again. She stilled at the sight of a flintlock pointed directly at them.

Tate pushed his mount forward, and Ava reached over, grabbing his arm. "He's armed, Tate, look," she said, edging her horse backwards.

"Damn," Tate mumbled, doing the same. It was too late to run and they were both out in the open, sitting targets, when one thought about such things.

The man raised the flintlock and she quickly turned her horse, knowing they needed to get as far away as possible. A shot rang out through the area and Ava's horse reared. She grappled for a hold, but couldn't, and then she realized it was not only her that was going to fall. Flying backwards, her horse lost her footing and toppled as well. Ava came down hard and a searing pain tore up her arm from her wrist to her shoulder.

Manny thankfully didn't land on her, but rolled next to her before regaining her footing again and standing.

The sound of a retreating horse echoed in the trees and then the comforting arms of Tate about her person as he kneeled beside her, his eyes wild with fear as he looked her over for a bullet wound or some kind of injury from her fall.

"I'm well. I merely fell, that is all." Ava went to stand and grimaced in pain when her arm rejected the movement."

"You're hurt," he said, helping to support her.

Ava tried to move her shoulder and found it well enough, but when she tried to move her wrist, pain shot through the joint. "My wrist, I think," she grimaced.

Tate ripped the cravat from about his neck and wrapped it about her wrist, attempting to limit movement. Ava couldn't help but glimpse Tate's exposed neck now that his cravat was about her wrist and for a moment she forgot about the man on the hill and the danger they could still be in.

She glanced over her shoulder to where she'd seen him last, but no one was there.

"He rode off the moment the gun went off. I'm so sorry to have put you in danger, Ava. I should not have had you chase him with me."

She shook her head as he helped her to stand. With her good arm she dusted down her riding attire and picked a few leaves and twigs out of her hair. "No one is to blame but him for what happened here today. Neither of us knew what he was going to do."

Tate did not look persuaded, but he helped her over to her horse, checking over Manny quickly, and giving her the all-clear of any wounds.

"Do you think you can ride?"

"I think so, but I'll need help getting up in the saddle." Within a moment of the words being spoken aloud, Tate scooped her up as if she were as light as air and sat her on the saddle.

He whistled for his own mount and adjusting her arm to be against her chest for the ride home. He hoisted himself up on his horse, giving her a lovely view of his bottom. "Thank you," she said, tearing her gaze away, but not before he caught her ogling his rear end.

"Come, we'll head back to your estate and I'll have a doctor sent for straight away. If the wrist is broken, he'll know what to do."

Ava hoped it wasn't so, and was merely a sprain. The ride home was uncomfortable, but the bandage about her wrist did help in some way to stop the hand from moving and jerking the joint.

Tate glanced at her often, his eyes shrouded with concern, and her heart warmed that he cared. It was nice the two of them being friends again. She had missed him more than she admitted even to herself. "You were always looking out for others. Even now, so many years since we first met and you're still a caring soul, no matter how much you may try to dissuade me of that fact."

"Not caring enough since you're injured." He frowned. "This is my fault," he said again, glancing at her hand that rested against her chest. "I should have gone after him by myself. Not placed you in danger as I did."

"What good would that do?" Ava retorted, not wanting to hear him blaming himself in the least. "We did not know the man was armed, or that he would run. I do believe we can agree that the gentleman was up to no good and could possibly be the man starting the fires."

He sighed, leaning over and supporting her back as the horses worked their way through an incline in the field. His warm hand against her spine sent shivers down it and she shut her eyes a moment, reveling in the feel of him again, of having him as close as he now was.

"I think you may be right. I suppose I shall be writing to the Runner again this evening."

Ava threw him a smile. "I think so." The ride home was slow. The weather took a turn for the worse, and when the sunlight disappeared behind a cloud, Ava regretted not bringing her heavier riding coat along with them.

"Are you cold?" he asked, pulling his horse to a stop. Ava did the same, looking up at the sky, it now looked like imminent rain.

"A little, but we should be home soon." Not that such a thing helped since in truth she was quite chilled. She shivered again and Tate jumped off his horse, walking over to her and hoisting himself up behind her.

She stilled at the movement as his body came to sit hard up against hers. They'd not been this close since the day before the planned elopement and she swallowed, unsure of a sudden, what to do with herself.

Tate was quiet a moment and she wondered what he was thinking. His body was tense, hard and broad, shadowed hers to a point, and she smiled as he leaned forward, taking the reins from her and kicking the mount forward.

His own horse followed.

The scent of sandalwood permeated the air about her and brought with it a flood of memories of when he had courted her. Of how she'd kissed his neck one time in the large hay barn at his estate and how she'd loved the woody, earthy scent ever since. He shifted behind her with each step of the horse and heat bloomed on her cheeks.

Using one hand to guide the horse, he wrapped his other arm about her waist, hoisting her harder against him. She gasped, and she could hear his rasping breath against her ear. Her own breath was ragged as if she'd run a footrace. In years past she would've turned, kissed him as they walked along, but now she could not.

As much as she hated to admit, Tate's mother was right. The man behind her needed a woman fit for the role of duchess and Ava, with her breeches and half boots covered in mud, her love of horses and racing would never suit the role. He needed a lady in the truest sense. She would never be one of those. Not really.

And yet, damn it all, a part of her wanted him with a fervor that chased any chill away. She was not suitable as a duchess, but that did not mean they could not come to some other kind of arrangement. One that was pleasant for them both.

Ava placed her hand over his and squeezed it a little. "I know you're worried, but truly, I think it's a sprain. I've had worse injuries coming off horses before, as well you know."

He growled his displeasure and surprisingly she felt the slightest touch of his lips against her hair. "I cannot lose you again. When I saw you fall, I thought you'd been shot, or that the horse would fall on you."

She rubbed his gloved hand, liking him comforting her more than she ought. This was bad. She should not allow such liberties, such intimate touching, but how could she refuse.

"I do not think he was a good shot."

He chuckled and the movement seeped into her soul,

lighting it up in ways it had not for many years. This time he did kiss her hair and tears sprung in her eyes. Ava put it down to the pain in her wrist, but it was not the reason. The man, his care, and sweet nature had always made her defenses crumble.

How would she deny herself him when she wanted him so very much? Just not the role of duchess.

Ava bit her lip, torn about it all.

The pull of Tate whenever she was around him grew stronger each day. More so than ever before, now that they knew the truth as to why they were separated in the first place. To ignore that pull was a battle she fought daily, and sometimes she didn't want to anymore. Sometimes she wanted to walk into his arms, lean up and kiss him like she used to and see where he would carry her.

To a future she'd once dreamed of, but had learned to live without.

~

*T*ate was in as much agony as Ava who now lay slumped against his chest. The sweet scent of rose wafted up from her hair and he breathed deep, the smell bringing up memories of days lazing about in the sun, simply talking or reading together.

Soon they would be home and he would have to move her. Have her shift from his arms and the thought did not bring comfort, only annoyance. He didn't want her to ever leave his arms again if he could help it, and the thought of how close she was, how both of them could have been killed today, made his muscles ache with tension.

The bastard who had shot at them could have killed her. He would not stop until the fiend was brought to book for doing such a thing. Tate was certain above anything else that the man who ran from them had something to do with the fire at his own estate and that of Lord Morton's.

No one innocent ran away from anything. They faced the issue and dealt with it, then and there.

"Tell me about France," he asked, needing to distract himself from having nearly lost her.

She looked over the land surrounding them, lost in thought a moment. "Southern France was beautiful, and the school had a small vineyard and we helped with the making of the wine sometimes. The headmistress was stern, but accommodating and as much as I missed Papa and home, I did make some wonderful friends, Hallie being one of them."

He pulled her closer to him, holding her against his chest, loving the fact she did not pull away or tense at the action, but simply melded into his embrace and welcomed it.

"What about you?" she asked, turning to look up at him. "What did you do in New York?"

Tate inwardly cringed at his antics in the great city. The nights of unlimited imbibing, the many ladies that had graced his bed, the horse races and gambling. The over-indulged future duke that was acting out against a girl he thought guilty of playing him the fool. When in truth, she had been as miserable as he. "I hate to remember what I was like, both in New York and London upon my return. I'm ashamed to think how I acted out against my circumstances that I wholly laid at your door." Tate met her gaze, her wide brown eyes watching him with no judgement. She should judge him. He'd been a rogue of the worst kind. "I'm so sorry," he whispered. "If I could change the past, I would."

She threw him a tentative smile. "It was not your fault and nor was it mine. We were tricked."

Tate lost himself in her gaze, the pull of her, the need that coursed through his blood at having her in his arms once more was too much to deny. Her eyes grew heavy, slipping to look at his lips and he leaned down, just as the shouts and laughter of someone nearby caught his attention. He glanced up and realized with a great deal of annoyance that they were back at Ava's estate.

Cursing the fact, he'd missed an opportunity to kiss her, he walked the horse on before stopping before the front door of Ava's home. A servant ran out with a candle now that the sun was dropping in the western sky. He jumped down and then helping Ava do the same, didn't give her a moment to walk, but simply scooped her back up again and started for the doors.

"Have Doctor Bradley sent for in Ascot immediately. Miss Knight may have broken her wrist."

The servant followed them indoors and bowed. "Of course, right away, Your Grace."

Without thought, he started up the stairs, ignoring the knowing giggle from Ava as he made the first floor landing. "I'll take you to your room and ensure you're tended."

She grinned, nodding without opposition. A maid came out of a room further along the corridor. She bobbed a quick curtsy, her eyes widening in shock at seeing Tate carrying her mistress.

"I can walk perfectly well, you know, duke," Ava said, the only person in the world he allowed to call him that. Even though the first time she did they were arguing with each other, but it did have a sweet, private notion about it, something just for them. "Do not worry, Jane," Ava said as they passed her maid. "The duke thinks I have broken my leg instead of my wrist."

He glanced down at her, not amused at her teasing. "Are you laughing at me, Miss Knight?" he asked, raising his brow.

"Always," she said. He placed her on her feet beside the bed, his attention not on their surroundings or the staff bustling about them, but Ava, only ever Ava.

Miss Evans rushed into the room, coming over to them. "What happened? I saw the duke carry you upstairs and I didn't know what to think?"

From her knowing look Miss Evans gave them both, Tate would wager she knew exactly what to think. He masked his amusement. "Miss Knight fell off her horse and landed heavily on her wrist. It may be broken."

"Oh, my dear," Miss Evans said, calling out instructions for the maid to prepare a cold compress and tisane for pain.

Another maid bustled into the room, pulling down the bedding for the night and going into the dressing room and coming out with a shift.

Miss Evans met his gaze and she smiled. "We will take care of Ava from here, Your Grace. Old friends you may be, but propriety must be upheld. Once she's settled and the doctor has called, I shall send word to you about her condition."

He nodded, looking back to Ava. "Miss Evans is right, but I will not return home. I'll wait downstairs until the doctor has left, and please do not hesitate to ask me for anything that you need." Her sweet, angelic face looked up at him and he had the overwhelming urge to clasp her cheeks and kiss her. Damn he longed to taste her sweet lips once more.

How many times while away had he dreamed of her, of being just so, alone in her room. No one to interrupt them or stop them from what they'd both desperately wanted before they parted. A couple of times they had both almost lost control of their emotions, but thankfully they had not. And yet now, five years later, the emotions she wrought inside of him, it only felt like a matter of time before they both combusted from them.

He lifted her uninjured hand and kissed her glove. "Good night," he said, walking from the room.

Tate strode down the passage heading for the stairs and the library below. He had to get hold of himself. There was no certainty that Ava even wanted him in the way that she had all those years ago. He might be dreaming up all her reactions to him, seeing and feeling things that were no longer there for her. His own yearning for more might be wholly on his own behalf and not be reciprocated.

He entered the library, which also acted as Ava's office, and slumped down in the leatherback chair before the well-stoked fire. A decanter of brandy sat on a table beside his seat and reaching for the crystal, he poured himself a glass.

Sipping his drink, he thought back over the day, all that had occurred. Once he knew of Ava's condition he would write to his Runner and also to Lord Morton to notify him as to why they had not arrived this afternoon. He would ride over there tomorrow and see how they fared, talk to the older gentleman and see if he could give any more details on the fire and if anyone saw anything not yet mentioned.

The thud of horse's hooves on the turf outside sounded and Tate stood, looking out the window to see the doctor pull up his horse before the door, Miss Evans going out to greet the elderly gentleman.

Tate stayed where he was knowing Miss Evans would have everything in hand. The fact he could not go into Ava's room, in any case, meant his presence was unwarranted. There was little doubt Ava would be dressed for bed and it would not be appropriate for him to attend.

He pushed the thought away, not needing to imagine what she looked like lying on her bed, hair cascading down her shoulders, her eyes heavy with sleep and reminiscent of what they looked like when she was thoroughly kissed.

Tate went back to the chair before the fire, sat, and settled in to wait for news.

When Ava had been hurt, the crippling fear that he could lose her had been telling indeed. If there had ever been any doubt that trying to win her love once more would be a mistake, today proved otherwise.

The moment she fell, Tate knew at once that he could not live without her. But could she live without him? That was a question he could not answer.

Certainly she reacted in his arms as she always had, and if he kissed her, there was little doubt in his mind that she would respond favorably. But that did not mean Ava wanted him for a husband.

There were certain times of the year that they would need to travel away from Berkshire to Town. Mingle and be seen, and of course he needed to attend the House of Lords. Upon marriage Ava, would become responsible for managing his many households, a mistress to hundreds of employees across all his estates. It was no mean feat, but Tate was certain she was capable. An intelligent, forward-thinking duchess was what he'd always wanted, if only she would give him a second chance.

With his hand in marriage, came responsibility. A duty that he wasn't convinced she wanted. Not now that she had tasted independence, and was answerable to no one but herself. Not that he would curb or box her into any sort of life and keep her under strict rule, but that didn't mean that Ava did not believe that being a duchess meant that anyway.

And if she did not have those worries before, his mother's words the other day to her would've most certainly placed them in her mind. Tate frowned, drinking down the last of his brandy. He had a lot of work ahead of him, and not including the rebuilding of his stables or catching the culprit who had burned them down, but winning back the love of his life...

CHAPTER 10

The next two days were a blur of pain and restless moments of sleep. No matter which way she moved in bed, or walked about the house, the action caused her hand to shift and therefore her severely sprained wrist to ache.

Ava rolled over in bed, the morning sunlight streaming into her room and pulling her from sleep. The sight of a male form sitting in a chair beside her bed pushed all sleep from her body. She sat up, cringing as her wrist protested the movement. "Tate, what are you doing in my room?" she looked about quickly, noting they were alone. "You should not be in here," she whispered.

Tate sat on a chair, a discarded book laying open in his lap. He leaned toward the bed, reaching for her hand. "I came early to watch Titan on the gallops and wanted to be here when you woke. I brought you up some breakfast," he stood and walking to a sideboard in her room, picked up the tray and placed it beside her on the bed. "How are you feeling?" he asked.

Ava adjusted herself on her pillows. "Other than my

wrist aching, the rest of me feels very well. The tisanes Hallie has been having made for me work very well. I'm not sure what she's having put in them, but whatever herb she's found is very beneficial. I'm thankful for her company." She glanced down at the bandaging about her wrist, her shift gaping a little at her throat. Ava clasped her blankets and pulled them up over her chest. Tate stared at her a moment, before he sighed, coming to sit on her bed.

"I was so scared there was more to the injury and I cannot tell you how thankful I am, you were not shot. The doctor says you will be fine, after a week or two of rest."

Leaning back on the pillows she could imagine what she looked like. A woman who'd been unable to do a lot for herself these past three days, and having just woken up, her hair would be askew, her eyes puffy from sleep. And yet, the look of utter adoration that she read on Tate's face reminded her of how he used to look at her when they were courting.

"Do you remember when you taught me how to swim?" she asked, watching him.

He smiled, nodding a little. "I do. You had me showing you all these different strokes that I was so worldly and knowledgeable about and all the while you already knew how to swim. I discerned in that instant you were trouble."

Ava chuckled, remembering he'd gone as red as a beet when she'd told him the truth of her ability. "You were so embarrassed and thought I'd tricked you. Which in a way I had, I suppose?"

He looked down at the bed, his finger following the line of the embroidered flowers on her bedding. "What made you think of that time?" he asked, looking up and catching her gaze.

The urge to run her hand over his jaw, shadowed with

the smallest amount of stubble was impossible to deny. He'd always been there for her, wanting to please and be her friend, a protector. "I don't know." She shrugged. "I've been thinking of our past a lot lately and that is but one of many memories that makes me smile."

"As good a swimmer as you professed to be, you were lucky I was there the day you had a cramp and went under, flailing about, if I recall." He grinned and she chuckled, although at the time it was far from amusing.

"There are going to be times in our lives when accidents or situations occur where we'll not be together. I wanted you to know that what happened to us three days ago was completely out of our control. You don't have to stay and keep watch over me, Tate. I'll be fine." Ava reached out and placed her hand over his, reveling in its warmth and that he turned his palm up and clasped her hand in return. "And anyway, is it proper that you're in here, Your Grace?" she asked, smiling mischievously.

His intense stare, loaded with too many emotions to deal with at this time bore into her. "Do you want me to leave?"

She thought on it only a moment. Ava shook her head, going against her better judgment, against her own promises, that she would forever be her own person. Answer to no one and be owned by none.

"I don't want you to go, no," she said at last, meaning every word.

"That is good, then," he said, leaning down and placing a soft kiss on her cheek. "Because I do not wish to leave," he whispered into her ear.

Ava shivered and turned, placing her lips close enough to kiss him. Her injured wrist forgotten, her attention snapped to his lips, still as soft and as tempting as they ever were. A fierce longing tore through her at having been denied him for so many years.

She wrenched back as the door opened and her maid came in with hot water and fresh linens.

Tate did not move for a moment, and then with a heavy sigh sat back. His intense stare left her breathless and she could feel her cheeks burning. What was he thinking after their almost kiss? Was he waiting for the maid to leave? Or was he simply debating whether to wait at all and kiss her anyway, spectators or no.

He leaned over and picked up her breakfast tray, placing it before her. "Thank you," she said, picking up her cup of tea, and taking a sip. Ava dismissed her maid, and also ignored Jane's startled visage at being asked to go. "I must admit that I feel ravenous this morning."

"So do I," he murmured, no mirth in his tone. "I will call on you tomorrow, Ava. There are some things that I need to discuss with the Bow Street Runner about the fire. He arrived today from London. Apparently there is the possibility that it's Lord Matthew Oakes, the viscount who's been starting the fires."

A cold shiver tore down her spine at the mention of Matthew, a man she never wanted to set eyes on again. A man she'd promised herself that she would never be a victim to again.

Ava reached out and clasped Tate's arm, halting his departure. "No wait, Tate. I mean, Your Grace. Are you sure it's Lord Oakes that you suspect? I thought he was in Spain."

"He was, but he returned only a week before the fire at Cleremore."

Ava gasped and he frowned, studying her a moment. "What do you know of Lord Oakes?"

Sickness pooled in her stomach at the thought of telling Tate what a fool she'd been only last year when she'd returned to England only to hear that Tate was in London, living life to the fullest with a bevy of women, all of whom were not her. That she'd acted out of jealousy and with her foolishness, a mistake that had almost cost her life and reputation.

"He is not to be trusted, that is all I know of him."

"You're lying, I can tell, Ava," he said, using her given name that startled her a little. "And please, allow me to call you by your given name and you in turn mine. I think we've known each other long enough to be on such terms when in private."

She met his gaze, liking that idea. "Very well, we shall go by our given names." Her answer was in part a way to stall answering the question he asked. How could she explain that town gossip had been like a knife to her heart and had made her foolish and blind? That she'd made a mistake that she could never take back again.

"I know Lord Oakes somewhat. Rumor has it he's in financial strife, but to start fires in the same county he resides in makes no sense. I do find it hard to believe that he would have anything to do with this matter. He never showed such cruelty towards animals that I ever saw." But she'd certainly seen his temper toward people, her in particular when he did not get his way.

The duke sat beside her again, and she shuffled back a little, his size and presence overwhelming her, muddling her mind, and she needed to keep her wits about her. Needed to remind herself that she didn't want a husband, that he didn't fit into her perfectly planned future as an old maid.

Ava picked up a piece of toast and took a bite, busying

herself as much as she could in the hopes that he'd forget this line of inquiry and go home.

"If you know anything about Lord Oakes, you need to tell me. I have not seen him since he was a boy in short coats and from what I can remember he was never any bother. But if you know anything that may explain why he's been possibly seen at Cleremore and now Lord Morton's estate, you must tell me."

Thinking back to the night of the duke's fire, the gentleman who'd yelled out notifying them of the second fire certainly sounded similar to Lord Oakes... Ava shook the idea aside. She was imagining things now. There was so much going on that night, so many people about, it could've been anyone, even one of the duke's own employees.

"I do not know anything," she said, pushing away her breakfast. Tate picked up the tray and placed it on the small table beside her bed.

"Ava," he said, tilting up her chin so she would look at him. "You can tell me anything. Please, it's important."

His beseeching pulled at a part of her only he had ever been able to reach and she sighed, ready to fall on her disgraceful sword one way or another. "This is only what I know of Lord Oakes' character. I have no knowledge or reason to suspect him of starting the fires about the county."

"Of course," he said, waiting patiently for her to begin.

Ava bit her lip, trying to find the right words to tell Tate of her shame. "Upon my return to England I returned to Berkshire to take over the estate here. I had heard you were living in London and what a life you were having."

Tate shifted on the bed and she smiled when a light

blush stole over his cheeks. Of whom he was enjoying and how many they totaled. Ava wanted to tell him how the news had ripped out her heart for a second time, but she could not. He could never know how much she'd missed him when she was not deluding herself. "I made a dreadful mistake, and one that I shall never be able to repair."

~

*T*ate waited patiently for Ava to tell him what she knew of Lord Oakes and the shame he recognized in her eyes gave him pause. He could not help but wonder what it was that she knew about the man that made her so uneasy. He'd not known she was well acquainted with his lordship at all, but her uneasiness when talking about him and her avoiding telling him what happened chilled his blood.

He shut his eyes a moment, hating the thought that she'd been courted by the gentleman. That she'd possibly cared for another person, enough so to form an attachment, even if that attachment was merely friendship. He didn't want her to be with anyone else. All his time abroad the very last thing he had thought of before he slept at night was her.

"Tell me, Ava." *Please* hovered on his lips but he bit the word back. She would tell him when she was ready.

"We met through the stables. At the time Lord Oakes had a thoroughbred, Majesty, that he wanted us to train up for racing. Prior to the gelding breaking down and being retired soon after, we formed a friendship. Well, at least I thought it was a friendship."

A hard knot formed in his gut, but he schooled his

features, not wanting to scare her. "And he believed it to be more than benign friendship?"

She met his gaze quickly before looking away. "He did, he thought that there could be more. He asked me to be his mistress. Said he was courting an heiress who would soon solve his financial troubles, but that she was a woman who preferred Town. A mistress in the country, not far from his estate would be favorable."

"Not his wife?" Tate clamped his mouth shut, lest his voice betray his disgust and loathing for Lord Oakes. The bastard wanted to use Ava as his whore. Rage consumed him and he clamped down on his temper, knowing it would not help in having Ava tell him the whole truth.

"No, not his wife." Ava fiddled with her blanket for a moment, lost in thought. "I thought myself for a time capable of such a thing. He is certainly handsome and seemed genuinely sweet, and as I had no intention of marrying, the idea of taking a lover wasn't wholly abhorrent to me. And so I agreed."

Tate stood, running a hand through his hair, a multitude of visions running through his mind. His head thumped and he thought he may be sick. "You gave yourself to him?" The words came out strained and he wasn't sure what he should do.

Ava remained silent a moment, her face pale. "No, it never went so far, but he did get very close. If it were not for my maid walking in after hearing an odd noise, he would have."

Shock and revulsion shot through him like a bullet and he went to her, sitting on the bed and taking her in his arms. "Ava, no." He held her tight, wishing he'd been here to protect her. She was stiff in his arms a moment and he sighed in relief when she relaxed and wrapped her arms about his waist, melding against him. "I'm so sorry, my darling."

He felt her shudder in his arms and to his shock he realized she was crying. "I'm so ashamed, Tate. I led him to believe that I wanted such a relationship, but when one afternoon he pressed for more I realized my mistake. I tried to explain, to apologize to him that I was mistaken, but he became so mad, so violent. The words he yelled at me were unlike any I've ever known and when I went to leave the room, he wouldn't allow it."

Tate rocked her slightly in his arms. All this time he had been in London, sleeping his way through the willing ladies of the *ton* and the woman who'd always had his heart, his beautiful, caring Ava had been assaulted. And he'd not been there to save her.

"I'm so sorry. I wish you had sent for me. I would've been here for you." And he would've killed Lord Oakes for his actions. And even if the blaggard was not proven to be the arsonist, he would still have his revenge on him regarding Ava. That, he could promise the bastard. He would call him out if he had to.

"No one knows," she said, pulling back a little, her eyes swollen and red. "No one can ever know. I've had to keep this to myself, a dirty, nightmare-inducing secret that could ruin all that my father and I have built. If any of the peerage found out that I even contemplated being his mistress…it could ruin me."

His heart ached for her that he could not fix her pain. He held her close, not ever wishing to let go. "I made my maid swear not to tell a soul and to this day she has not."

He wiped the tears that slipped down her cheek. "You have nothing to be ashamed of, Ava. His actions toward you were his own and say everything about what kind of man he is and what type of moral code he abides by. You had nothing to do with his choices. People are allowed to change their minds there is no law against that."

She smiled through her tears, reaching up to lay her hand over his that still touched her cheek. "Thank you for saying that. I do try and think that way, to push down the horror of that afternoon, but sometimes it is hard."

"Never give in to such thoughts for they only give Lord Oakes power over your mind. And if there is one thing I know about you that I admire and adore equally, it is your mind and the fierceness that simmers in your soul. You're a good person, Ava. What happened to you was not."

Even as children she'd been the kindest person he'd known, and it was possibly why from the moment he'd met her down by the river where they had swum together from that day forward, he'd gravitated toward her.

His parents' marriage was amicable enough, but his mother was a hard, often cold and unforgiving duchess. His father was simply never there and so the family life, the connection between parent and child that Ava had with her papa had been new and amazing to him. He'd wanted that himself, and as soon as they were friends, Ava's father had enfolded him into their pack of two and made them a pack of three.

"This happened after your father had passed?" Tate couldn't believe what he was hearing. He stood and walked over to Ava's desk near the window in her room, and poured himself a glass of water. His stomach churned and threatened to cast up his accounts. He ought to call him out. Put a bullet between his eyes and let him rot in the woods. To know Ava had been carrying around this burden on her own brought such guilt to course through his body that it near crippled him. After loving her as wildly as he did, he should've returned to Berkshire and ensured she was cared for after her father's passing. He should've ensured her safety, no matter her choice regarding her future whether it be with him, someone else or no one at all.

"I had no one to call him out, you see. As you know I have no siblings, and with father gone I simply had to live with the torturous memory of how close I came to being ruined. To hear that he could possibly be the man who is starting the fires about the county, well," she shook her head, her eyes downcast. "I never wanted to see him again, you see, but I fear, with this new development, that may change."

It was more than despicable and Tate couldn't help but wonder why Lord Oakes would act out in such a violent way. Was he ill of mind, or simply angry at his neighbors and their successes that he had not gained himself in the racing world? Or was it Ava and her refusal of his lordship's proposition.

"The selfish part of me does not want to face him again. Do you think I'm a coward for saying that?" she asked, meeting his gaze. Fear lurked in her dark, brown orbs and his heart went out to her. He could understand Ava not wanting to see Lord Oakes. It did not mean that he could not face his lordship. Call him out, put a bullet through his head, and solve all their problems. "I'm going to kill him," he mumbled to himself.

Ava gasped and Tate cringed, knowing she'd heard what he'd said. She pushed the bedding back and came over to where he stood near the windows.

Ava clasped his arm and pulled him to face her. "You will do no such thing, Tate. It's illegal to duel to start with. If he is the man that has been causing all these fires, then we will deal with him through the law and we need to do it without him knowing. There is no proof of what he did to me and although he tried, he did not succeed with his assault. If he finds out we suspect him of the crimes at your estate and Lord Morton's, he will ruin me in Society and he'll take pleasure in doing so."

"I cannot let him get away with what he did to you."

Her grip eased and she slid her hand down his arm to clasp his hand. "And we won't. I know financially he has very little left. He's had to sell off land around his estate to the point that all that remains is his home and an acre or two that surrounds it. Seeing him go down for this crime as a fire starter and murderer is good enough for me. He can do no harm to any property, stable hands or woman again if he's in Newgate."

"It's not good enough for me though, Ava." He stepped toward her and clasped her cheeks in his hands. "He tried to take what was not freely given. I cannot allow him to get away with such a heinous crime."

Her eyes filled with tears and his loathing of Lord Oakes doubled.

"I know you want to defend my honor, and I'm thankful for that. I truly am. We've known each other for so long, Tate. But it's not your job to save me. I will not let you put yourself in harm's way for something I prefer to forget. Please, leave it in the past, where it belongs."

The physical scars may have healed for Ava, but the mental scars still remained after what the viscount had done to her, and so no, he would get his revenge on this bastard, whether or not he was the culprit behind the arson attacks.

He sighed, letting the conversation drop. She was still injured and didn't need to be thinking of her attacker or

Tate's actions against him at this time. "Come," he said taking her hand and pulling her back towards the bed. "You need your rest. And I promise I shall not do anything until we have a chance to talk about all this further, when you're better."

Tate helped her back under the covers, puffing up the pillows behind her head and pouring her another cup of tea before handing it to her. "I will leave you now and let you get your rest. I will return this evening, maybe we could dine together in here."

She glanced at him mischievously. "Do you think that's wise, Your Grace? Your reputation as a libertine is well and truly fixed in London. You really shouldn't be dining in my bedroom."

He shook his head at her ability to be sweet and funny, especially now that he knew she'd been hurt. In all truth he should not be in her room now, no matter later to dine with her, but first and foremost they were friends and if she were too sore to come downstairs to eat, well then, he would come upstairs instead. "I will be back to dine and be damned what Society says about that."

He left her then, heading downstairs and out the door, needing to get on horseback as fast as possible. Within a few minutes he was galloping back toward his estate, but he wouldn't return too soon. Tate needed to clear his head, calm his blood, and plan on the downfall of Lord Oakes. He pushed his horse on, jumping a hedgerow before slowing to cross a small stream. Ava would have justice and he would make sure she did.

If he enjoyed meting out such justice, then all the better for it.

CHAPTER 11

I'm free from what I once felt for you. I wish you all the very best in whatever direction your life takes you and hope that no matter what, that you are happy...

— An Excerpt from a letter from Miss Ava Knight to the Duke of Whitstone

A week later Ava, with her wrist still bandaged, met Hallie in the hall who was taking the mail from a servant.

"Anything in there for me?" she asked, ordering tea and going into the library where there was sure to be a pile of letters and work that she'd neglected the past week after spraining her wrist. Considering how sore it was only two days ago, she was surprised today it was feeling reasonably well. Of course she didn't have full movement back yet, but it was definitely a marked improvement.

The daily visits from Tate had also aided her healing, both of her injury and her heart, making her self-inflicted tenet to never marry, to never seek a partner in life even more difficult to abide. So many times she'd caught herself contemplating them. Caught herself watching as he read to her poetry and gothic novels that they both enjoyed, wondering if marriage to him, being a duchess, would still allow her the freedom she had now. Or would she have to compromise somewhat on her independence? Would Tate in turn allow her to do the same for what was expected of her as a duke's wife?

"There is a letter from Willow," Hallie said, breaking the seal and scanning the note quickly. "She wants us to come to London for a week or two. To attend some balls that she's been invited to by her great-aunt through marriage, the Viscountess Vance." Hallie sat on a nearby settee and continued to scan the note. "She says something here about the little season coming to an end and wants us there with her before they leave for the viscountess' country estate."

Ava went to her chair behind her desk and sat, rummaging through her letters that were neatly piled before her. "I forgot Willow had a titled aunt. Does it say if her ladyship is happy for us to attend with them?"

Hallie scanned the note further. "Yes, it states here that she looks forward to meeting Willow's friends from school, and that we're welcome to stay at her townhouse in Berkley Square." Hallie glanced up, her eyes bright with excitement.

It was a lovely invitation and one that even Ava would never turn down. Not that she particularly wished to attend London events over a week or two, but Willow was one of their best friends in the whole world, and if she'd asked for them to come and keep her company, well then, Ava would do so of course.

"I will inform my maid to pack our things and ready us for departure next week."

"What about your wrist?" Hallie asked, folding the letter away.

Ava shrugged. "It'll be healed more so by next week, and gloves will hide the bruising that remains. If anyone does see the injury I will simply tell them the truth that I fell off my horse. No one will question me further on it."

Hallie leaned back in her chair, studying her a moment. Ava picked up the letters and busied herself sorting and opening them. When Hallie went quiet, like she was right now, it only meant that her mind, sharp and all-too-knowing, was churning to ask something.

"What about the duke?"

Ava shrugged, reading a letter from her feed supplier in Ascot. "What about the duke? I'm sure he's more than capable of keeping himself busy while we're away." Ava smiled at her friend, determined to evade her questioning.

"You know that's not what I meant." Hallie raised her brow, nonplussed.

"He's just returned from town and you're mistaken if you think he'll return to London simply because we've been invited down for a few days."

Hallie chuckled, shaking her head. "I think that if anyone is going to be mistaken it'll be you. The man is smitten with you, and you know it. Why, the day he carried you into the hall after your fall, well, he looked like a man about to have an apoplectic fit. The fear etched on his face over your injury wasn't merely neighborly concern, he was panicked that it was possibly more severe than it turned out to be, thankfully."

The mention that the duke was so very worried for her left a warm, comforting feeling to settle in her soul. She bit her lip, unable to hide the smile that formed on her lips. She shook the thought aside, reminding herself that she didn't want him courting her, forming an understanding with her again. He needed to marry a woman suitable for a duke. A woman who actually wanted the position and all the trappings that came with it.

~

A week later, Ava stepped out of the viscountess' carriage with the help of her ladyship's coachmen and followed Viscountess Vance and her friends up the steps of Earl Tinley's townhouse. The ball this evening was rumored to be a most sought after event in London due to the fact that their host was distantly related to King George IV. Everyone who was anyone wanted to be in attendance, Viscountess Vance and her friends were no exception.

Not that the King would attend such an event, even for distant relatives, but it did make for an interesting conversation. The ballroom was alight with hundreds of wax candles, giving the room a golden, magical glow. The musicians were situated on a small balcony that overlooked the ballroom. They played a minuet and some of the guests already present were dancing while others watched on, chatting and mingling with their set.

Tonight Ava wore a gown of gold silk, and her mother's pearls that her ladyship's maid, a master with the latest designs that Ava's own maid had been happy enough to learn from, had artfully woven the jewels throughout her dark locks. Thankfully her silk gloves hid her hands and bruised wrist, not to mention her nails that were not as well kept due to her constant horse work.

She smiled when Hallie placed her arm through hers, her friend all but bouncing with expectation.

"How exciting this is, Ava. It has been so long since we've been in such company, if we ever were. I can tell you that they do not have balls such as these in Egypt."

They did not, Hallie was right about that. Keeping pace with the viscountess who was heading for the opposite side of the room, Ava noticed a few curious looks from those present, and nodded hello to those she knew through the racing world.

Interestingly enough, some of the glances they gained were appreciative and curious, and for the first time ever Ava set out to enjoy her time in London.

They stopped beside a well-lit hearth, a gold embossed mirror the size of the chimney sat above the mantle and reflected the light and the guests. Everything about the room screamed privilege, and looking about she couldn't help but think of Tate.

This was his world, his life. Such furniture, excess and wealth that was on show, the jewels, imported silk dresses and men's finery, the *ton*, and manner of speech, were all part of a life he was used to living within.

Ava glanced across the room and spied the dowager duchess of Whitstone talking with a group of matrons, no doubt all of them titled and married to some peer. She hadn't realized the dowager would be back in town, considering she'd only recently arrived in Berkshire. Her grace spotted her and turning her nose up into the air, gave her the cut direct.

Ava shouldn't have expected anything less, but still, the affront stung.

"Here is a glass of champagne for you, Ava. Drink it, it's all deliciousness."

She laughed, taking the flute from Willow. "Thank you," she said, turning away from the dowager and the few women about her that had looked over toward her at the same time. Ava wasn't naive enough not to know Tate's mother was spreading her vicious lies about her. She pushed the disappointment away that they could not even be civil toward each other and set out to enjoy the ball instead.

The years she'd spent in school in France had not allowed for such outings. They had not been able to partake in dances and balls that the peerage living in France partook in. Quite often they had only each other for company. Their isolation from the outside world, only ensured that their friendships had morphed into something stronger than stone.

It was a shame that Evie and Molly were not here. They would enjoy a night such as this.

A gentleman bowed before Ava and the viscountess. He was an attractive man, of Ava's age, she would presume. His hair, even though quite short, suited him. He was a little shorter than Tate, but still taller than Ava, which she liked, but it was his eyes, they were amused and kind-looking, a feature Ava often looked for when meeting new people. You could tell a lot by looking into the soul of a person.

"Lady Vance, may you do me the honor of introducing me to your friends?"

The viscountess smiled, gesturing toward them as she made the introductions. "My niece, Miss Willow Perry, and her friends Miss Ava Knight and Miss Hallie Evans. This, dear girls, is the Marquess of Harlan."

Ava dipped into a curtsy and his lordship looked each of them over with an appreciative glance. "Pleased to meet you all. And Miss Knight, if you're not otherwise engaged, would you care to dance a cotillion with me?"

Ava glanced at Hallie and with her nod of approval, she held out her hand. "I would like that very much. Thank you, my lord."

He took her hand and placed it on his arm, leading her out onto the ballroom floor. "You're from Berkshire, I understand. Is there not a very well renowned racing stable there that goes by the name Knight?" he asked, maneuvering them expertly through the throng.

"I, yes, there is. My father had bred and trained horses prior to his death. I now run Knight Stables."

His steps slowed and he chuckled, looking down at her again. "Ah ha, so it is the famous female horse trainer that everyone is talking about. You're highly recommended. Did you know that?" He pulled her forward and it took Ava a moment to dampen down the pride that filled her, knowing their stables were so well regarded.

"Thank you, my lord. I'm happy to hear it is so. We certainly do our best to breed and train up the best racehorses that we can." Of course, some horses would never win any races, but with their breeding it did not mean that they could not produce one. A mistake some trainers had made by selling off horses that could very well produce a champion. Something Ava and her father refused to do unless they had tested the horse on the racetrack.

They settled into their positions for the dance and Ava looked about, taking in the grandeur. It was highly unlikely she would return to town after this week, certainly not to partake in the Season, and so she would enjoy this opportunity, if only so it gave her more contacts within the *ton* so they might use her stables, should they like to own a thoroughbred in the future.

The dance was pleasant and even though Ava hadn't taken part in a cotillion for some years, the steps she had learned from her dance master as a young woman were something she'd not forgotten. Over the next hour she danced two more dances with other gentlemen, and stood with the viscountess when Hallie and Willow too danced.

The evening was surprisingly enjoyable, considering she disliked such events and had never gone out of her way before to participate in them.

Ava sipped her wine while she waited for her friends to return from their dance sets when a cold shiver stole down her spine. Looking to her left she spied Lord Oakes staring at her with icy amusement.

Her skin prickled and she shivered having hoped to never see his face again. The image of him, pushing her down into the settee's cushions, his painful, punishing grip on her arms as he held them behind her back, holding her still bombarded her mind and she fought not to be sick.

What was he doing here? He started toward her and she fought to pull all her defenses around her for the forthcoming confrontation. He bowed, smiling, the perfect gentleman for all Society to see. But Ava knew what lurked behind his cool, pretty visage. It was as ugly as the devil himself, and just as cruel.

"Miss Knight, how lovely to see you here in town. I have missed our rendezvous."

She glanced back toward the dancers, wishing the set would be over already so she would not be alone with him. "I fear, Lord Oakes, that your pining has been misplaced, for I have not felt the loss of your presence in any way." If anything, she'd hoped that he would be hurt in some carriage or riding accident. But alas, he was as healthy as the last time she had seen him.

He clasped his chest in mock injury. "You have not? I thought you would've missed our last joining most of all." He leaned toward her, closer than he ought and she stilled, fear spiking through her. "I know I still think of that time. How hot you made me. Why even now I grow hard at the thought of you compliant and beneath me, mewing and writhing in pleasure."

Ava refused to look at him and she let out a breath when he pulled away. She would not answer his taunt. He was not worthy of anything from her.

"Come now, my dear. We're friends, are we not? Come dance with me." He took the liberty of grabbing her injured wrist, spiking pain up her arm. She gasped and tried to pull her arm free without causing a scene.

"We are not friends and I do not wish to dance, my lord." When he let her go, she started back toward the viscountess, hoping she'd reach her presence before Lord Oakes caught up to her.

He clasped her wrist again, sensing an injury and squeezed, hard. Ava took a furtive glance about the room and heat stole across her skin when she noticed a few guests watching their every move. Lord Oakes, sensing the same, let her go, smiling sweetly. "Do as you're told, Ava darling. I would hate for London to find out that you contemplated being my mistress."

She rounded on him. "How dare you?" she whispered fiercely. "It would be wise to keep away from me, Lord Oakes, before you are the one that London turns their back on."

He laughed, throwing back his head as if she'd told an overwhelmingly amusing tale. "You're nothing but a horse trainer. Who do you think the *ton* will believe? A peer of the realm, or a whore from Berkshire."

"They will believe me."

The sound of Tate's voice brought tears to her eyes and she blinked quickly, not wanting Lord Oakes to see how relieved she was that Tate had rescued her. That Tate had seen Lord Oakes' treatment of her and had come to remove him from her presence vanquished her misery, and she was glad of his company. She threw him a tentative smile, always her protector.

The duke took her hand and placed it on his arm. "You come within an inch of Miss Knight again and I will call you out," the duke said, taking a step toward Lord Oakes and making him step back, "and put a bullet through your thick skull. Do you understand?"

Lord Oakes' eyes widened, and glancing at Ava nodded once. "We are in agreement, Your Grace," he sneered.

Tate pulled Ava out onto the dance floor as the first strains of a waltz started to play. "Are you all right, Ava? When I saw Lord Oakes starting toward you I could not get to you fast enough. I'm sorry you had to listen to that bastard."

The steps of the waltz allowed them to speak intimately, and not for anything could Ava take her eyes off him. He was such a good man, even with his ducal title and all his lands and money, he was still better than anyone she'd ever known. Her friend, first and foremost, and tonight he'd been her hero.

"Thank you, Tate. Dreadfully embarrassing to admit that had you not come I think I would've broken down in front of everyone."

His thumb brushed her shoulder through the silk of

her gown and she wanted his touch elsewhere. Wanted to feel his strength, his security that he always made her feel more than anything in the world. Under normal circumstances she was a strong woman, capable of running a successful business within an industry that was wholly male. She was accepting of her own company and that she would never marry or have children. A decision she was content to live with.

But being in Tate's arms again, under his protection also had its advantages. She'd forgotten what it was like to be loved, cared for and protected. Not that she believed Tate still in love with her, but he certainly cared enough to seek her out. His appearance in town could not be for any other reason other than that she was here. The knowledge left a warm, a safe feeling washing over her. Ava threw herself into the dance, wanting to enjoy every moment she could in his arms.

"I will never allow him to hurt you again. You have my word on that."

$\sim$

Tate drew Ava close, hoping that his face did not betray the seething rage that boiled inside of him. He would kill Lord Oakes if it were the last thing he did on this earth. Having walked into the ballroom, greeting guests, he had spotted Ava almost immediately.

She was like a spike of summer sun, glowing brightly within a sea of gray skies. He'd been caught by some acquaintances, but the moment he'd seen Lord Oakes sidle up beside her and the despair on Ava's visage, he knew his lordship was being inappropriate.

He'd left his group without a word and started for her

immediately. Typical of a bully's character, Lord Oakes had scuttled off when Tate threatened him. But he would have him pay. A man such as Lord Oakes was a menace, an untrustworthy, vicious man that had he been a dog would've been put out of his misery long ago.

Without care, he pulled Ava closer than he ought, wanting to hold her completely and ensure to himself that she was well. "Do you wish to speak about what happened?" He met her gaze and was thankful that she seemed a lot calmer than when the dance first started.

"Not particularly. All I'll say about Lord Oakes is that I do not wish to see him again, in Town or in Berkshire."

He nodded, wanting that for her as well. "I have a meeting with the Bow Street Runner tomorrow morning. Would you care to sit in on the meeting? He has some information to impart apparently. His letter I received yesterday was quite adamant that I meet with him as soon as may be."

"Do you think someone has seen who has been starting the fires? Even if it is not Lord Oakes, I would, of course, like to see whoever is the fire-starter be brought to justice."

"As would we all." They were quiet a moment as he maneuvered them around some other participating couples. "Ava, I need to speak to you about what happened at Cleremore regarding my mother. After the dance, would you be willing to take a turn about the terrace with me?"

A small frown marred her brow but after a moment she said, "Of course. I think we need to discuss that as well."

He nodded and set out to enjoy the dance. Every so often he caught glimpses of Lord Oakes skulking about the room and Tate's temper notched ever higher. How dare the bastard show his face in Society? Now that Tate knew what he'd done, and what he could possibly be doing in relation to the fires, the fiend deserved to be ostracized from London Society forever, from England, for that matter.

The dance came to a regrettable end and taking Ava's hand, he led her toward the French doors that were open for the evening and escorted her outside. The air was not cold, considering the time of year, and yet the sweet, fresh country smells that assailed them in Berkshire were not to be found. Here, the air had a hint of coal dust in it, along with the smell of burning wood from the indoor fires. Surprisingly and with some relief, there were no other couples on the terrace to interrupt their discussion and Tate didn't want to share Ava with any of London Society, in any case. He wanted her all to himself, now and forever.

He took Ava's hand and placed it on his arm, walking her toward the steps that lead down onto the lawn and garden beyond. From here, he could see a small wooden structure in the garden that, in the moonlight, revealed it was covered in ivy. They ambled without haste, happy to be in each other's company.

"I want to talk to you about what my mother said the other day that I know you heard." It had bothered him the moment he'd returned to the parlor to find Ava gone. That his mother had made her feel unwelcome was not something he'd allow her to feel. Not without her knowing that he did not feel the same.

She flicked away a stray strand of hair that had fallen over her eye, placing it behind her ear. "You have nothing to apologize for, Your Grace. It is no secret your Mother has never liked me and I can understand that she wants someone suitable for you to marry. If I were titled, had multiple properties that I had to produce heirs for, I too would be concerned if my son who had inherited a dukedom had been showing an unwavering preference to a woman of no rank who has little to recommend her but for the horses she breeds."

He pulled her to a stop, meeting her gaze. "You must know that I think more of you than someone who trains and breeds racehorses. I do not care what my mother thinks. All I care about is that I right the wrong committed against us five years' ago and that you give me some indication that you might possibly be mine again."

She walked ahead of him and he followed her, unsure of what she was thinking. They came upon the structure covered with ivy and Ava went inside, seating herself down on a small wooden bench that was placed in the middle of the space.

"My thoughts on marriage have changed, Tate. Surely you've seen that I do not need the sanctity of marriage to be happy, a successful businesswoman?" She glanced at him, her eyes troubled. "It's not something I need in my life. Do not make me deny you. I don't want to hurt you."

Her words drove panic to course through his blood and he came to sit by her side, willing her to see that had their parents not separated them all those years ago they would've been married right now. Possibly parents to a horde of children, running two great racing estates, happy.

"Being near you again has been like waking up from a nightmare. My life has been nothing but meaningless nothings and mistakes. I don't want to live like that anymore. I want you in my life as my wife, my lover, and my best friend."

"Tate," she whispered, shutting her eyes for a moment. "There are expectations for a duchess that I cannot rise to. I'm so set in my ways now, the racing stables that alone take up most of my spare time. As your wife, we would be required to travel to Town, entertain, be present during the sitting of Parliament. When will any of that leave room for my responsibilities? It would not."

"Of course, being my wife, a duchess comes with responsibilities, but you never shied away from them before, do not let what others say, what you believe will occur to dismiss the possibility of us together entirely."

She bit her lip, her brow furrowed. "Can we not be as we are, with no pressure and we'll see what happens? There is much that I need to consider, to think about."

Tate ran a hand over his jaw, wishing that they'd never been parted. That the time had not given way to Ava having to face things alone. He'd wanted to be there with her when she made decisions, support and push her in her endeavors. He would do as she asked, give her time, prove his loyalty, his love and he hoped to win her heart back?

"I will do anything that you ask of me," he said, meaning every word to the very core of his soul.

She turned toward him on the bench, her beautiful innocent eyes searched his gaze for a moment and heat spiked through his blood at the resolve he read in her dark brown orbs. She reached out and clasped the lapels of his jacket running her hands up his chest. He shut his eyes reveling in her touch and yet it was not enough. He wanted more, so much more. "More than anything right at this moment I want you to kiss me, Tate."

His body roared with need and he was desperate to kiss her. The years fell away and clasping her jaw in his hands he tilted her face, leaned down and took her lips. He sighed at the taste of her again, her soft, pliant lips that he remembered and had craved for so long.

Her hands fisted into his superfine coat, holding him firmly, but he wasn't going anywhere. He would never leave her again if she'd only choose him. Tate lost himself with each brush of her tongue, her soft sighs and little nips upon his lips that teased and hauled him back into her life.

The kiss was as if they had never parted at all. As if time had stopped. He hauled her hard against him, and her soft moan set alight his desire. The kiss deepened, changed, became more savage and raw. No matter what Ava told him, her kiss told him something completely different. She still wanted him with as much fire and need as he did her, and that gave him hope.

She belonged in his arms, his life.

"I've missed you so much," he said, kissing her neck, paying homage to her earlobe, knowing how much she enjoyed it.

She shivered in his arms, wrapping her arms about his neck. "I missed you too," she whispered against his lips.

He kissed her again and she moaned, and Tate took the opportunity to pull her closer still. They had never been so intimate before, but somehow now that they were older, wiser perhaps, such a closeness seemed natural, the next step for them.

Tate reminded himself Ava was an innocent, a woman who had already been through so much, and the last thing he wished to do was frighten her, or push her to a point that she was not ready for. And then she moved, placing herself all but in his lap and fire burst through his blood. He stilled a moment, at a loss to what she was doing and then she moved, undulating against his rigidness and he fought not to lose himself like an untried lad of eighteen.

"What is it that you're making me feel?" she asked, clasping his nape and meeting his eyes. Hers were glassy, bright and full of longing.

Tate's lips lifted in a half smile. "Desire, need."

"Ah," she said, nodding a little and undulating a little harder against his engorged member. He clamped his jaw, fighting the temptation to hike up her skirts and take her out here in the garden. "I like it," she whispered against his ear, the breath of her words firing his blood even more.

"I like it too," he growled, his hands flexing on her hips and helping her in her exertion.

The sound of laughter and clinking of glasses floated to them through the ivy and she stilled. It was all the warning they needed to know they were no longer so alone. Tate reluctantly untangled them, and set Ava away from him. In the little moonlight they had in the pergola he checked that her gown was back to rights, and that her hair was not mussed from the kiss. She grinned up at him as he took one last inspection of her appearance and his heart squeezed. He adored her and he could not lose her a second time.

"Do I look like I've been well kissed, duke?" she asked. She did look like she'd been kissed within an inch of her life in fact, and it made him only want to kiss her again. He would of course, but the next time it would be in a more private setting.

"I think we should stay here for a few minutes until we're both less conspicuous." And hopefully the few minutes' away from the ball would allow Ava's lips to return to their normal size, not a little swollen and ruddy from their exertions.

She reached up and settled his own hair back into place, before adjusting his cravat and waistcoat, ensuring all sat exactly as they should on his person.

"There," she said, nodding once. "That is better. Now you too do not look so ravished either."

The sound of the couples on the terrace quietened and

Tate took the opportunity to look out through the ivy, pleased to see that they had gone back indoors. "Come," he said taking her hand and pulling her towards the terrace. "I think it is safe to return to the ball now." Without any trouble he returned Ava back to Viscountess Vance and greeted her friends who waited patiently beside her ladyship when Ava introduced him to them. He had not met Miss Perry and her widened eyes at the sight of him led him to believe she'd not met many dukes in her life. "When are you returning to Berkshire?" he asked, before taking his leave.

"We are here a week, Your Grace," Ava replied. "Willow was kind enough to invite us to town to take part in the few events left during the little season. I must admit it's been a nice distraction from the troubles we've been having in Berkshire."

Which reminded Tate of what he needed to appraise Ava before he left the ball. "The meeting with the Bow Street Runner is at eleven tomorrow morning at my home in Grosvenor Square. Do you think you'll be in attendance? As a landowner in the area, I think it is important if you attend."

"Ava told us of your troubles, Your Grace," Willow said, lowering her voice to ensure privacy. "If there is anything that you need me or Miss Evans to do, please do not hesitate to ask."

"Thank you, Miss Perry. I will keep that in mind."

Ava smiled at her friend before turning back toward him. "Of course I shall attend. We're staying with her ladyship and I shall ask if I can take a maid with me."

"You can take Betsie with you, Ava. She is my maid," Miss Perry said.

Tate liked Ava's friends more and more. They both

seemed level-headed, intelligent and loyal. All traits he himself looked for in his own lifelong friendships.

"Thank you," Ava said. "You're being very kind."

Tate clasped Ava's hand and bowed over it. "Until tomorrow then, Miss Knight."

She threw him a secretive little smile that made him count the hours until he saw her again.

"Until tomorrow Your Grace."

~

*A*va rapped with the brass knocker on the door of the duke's residence at 11 o'clock sharp. A footman answered the door, his red livery coat and breeches adorned with gold buttons were a beacon of the wealth and power which resided inside these great walls.

Ava had never been to Tate's London residence, and its imposing, large size made her feel insignificant and common. Of course Tate's Berkshire property was large, but not as imposing as this home. Here the floor was marble and polished so much so that one could almost see their reflection. A wide, winding staircase stood center in the entrance leading up to the many rooms above. This floor too had multiple doors opening onto it, each one framed by two pillars that too looked to be made of marble.

So much grandeur and expectation sat on the shoulders of whoever lived here. A position she hesitated to accept. She took a fortifying breath, and shuffling out of her pelisse handed it to the waiting footman, along with her bonnet.

"The duke is expecting you, Miss Knight. If you would

follow me, please," a butler said, stepping out of the shadows and startling her a little.

His severe frown and disapproval at her arrival made Ava dared not do anything other than what he requested. Two chairs sat inside the door to the library. He pointed at them as if she could not see them well enough on her own. "You and your maid may sit there," the butler said, his severe countenance not budging an inch.

Ava took in the room as she entered. Tate's desk was situated central in the space. At one end, banks of mahogany shelves were full to the brim with books and scrolls, all of various shapes and sizes. The front windows overlooked the street, and carriages and people bustled by on their outings.

"Your Grace." Ava stood, dipping into a curtsy when Tate strolled into the room. His steps faltered a moment before dismissing the butler, he came over to her, smiling.

Tate nodded in greeting, pulling her toward the chair that sat opposite his desk. "Thank you for coming," he said, squeezing her gloved hand a little.

All thoughts of keeping her distance, of reminding herself that this was not the life she longed for any more vanished as he grinned down at her. Now there was nothing she'd like to do more than to kiss him again. The only thing stopping her was her maid and that the Bow Street Runner was due to arrive at any moment.

He leaned forward and kissed her cheek instead, and heat bloomed on her cheeks knowing Willow's maid would've seen his affection. The maid cleared her throat and Tate merely chuckled, giving her a devilish grin as she sat.

"I would be perfectly happy to kiss you fully, my dear. I no longer care that servants might see my regard for you. I will not hide my affection any longer. I have already spent too many years doing what others thought was best for us and I will not do it anymore." Ava glanced up at him as he stepped back and leant against his desk, arms folded over his chest.

Today Tate was dressed in tan breeches and knee high boots. His waistcoat, shirt and cravat were expertly tailored and his coat fit him like a kid glove. In this setting, this grand home and perfectly attired clothing, Tate was duke to his core. Powerful, charismatic and so above her reach, or at least he should be. He was too aristocratic for her common blood and deserved a woman who brought fortune and connections to his family. They had been so young, so immune to what was expected of them when they had planned to run away. Ava could see now that although there was a spark between them, a fuse that ignited each time they touched, that did not mean they were suitable to become husband and wife. As much as it pained her to admit, she was not his social equal, and should she marry him, the *ton* and Society at large would let him know that his choice was considered beneath him.

"While I will not put your reputation in jeopardy by declaring my intentions, but here in my office away from the prying eyes of meddling family members and matrons of the *ton*, I will kiss you if I want. I will kiss you for as long as you wish me to," he whispered, so the maid did not hear.

Ava bit her lip. How on earth would she deny him anything when he spoke to her in such a way? After last night and their kiss she'd thought of little else but doing it again, but that did not help either of them. Her life was in Berkshire, and his life was London, the House of Lords, Society and overseeing his many estates. A duke would expect his wife to be by his side, a pillar in Society, a hostess during the Season. How could a woman who bred racehorses and trained them to be champions do everything that was expected of her? She could not.

"Tate, I need your opinion on a subject that has been troubling me."

"Of course," he said. "Ask me anything, Ava?"

She met his gaze and forced the words she dreaded to know the truth of through her lips. "If we were to marry, what would be expected of me?"

He frowned, kneeling before her and taking her hand. "I would want to show you off. Bring you to London and shout it from the dome of St Paul's Cathedral that you're mine and no one else's. I would cover you in jewels, diamonds and gifts that would bring out the stunning color of your eyes and sweetness of your soul. And we shall dance, and make love until we no longer have the energy to do so. And that is to start."

His words sent panic through her of all such a promise would mean to her. "You would want to spend the Season each year here in town?"

He nodded. "Of course, we would have to travel to London often as I'm a member of the House of Lords and so Parliament brings me here regularly. As the Duke of Whitstone, it's expected that I'm seen during the Season, to attend balls and parties. My friends, which will become our friends will expect and want us to attend their gatherings."

He smiled, his eyes full of hope and unable to tell him how much his words dashed all her optimism, she smiled a little, running her hand over his jaw. "Tate…"

. . .

A fast rap at the door brought Tate to his feet before the butler entered, introducing the Bow Street Runner and thankfully stopping Ava from having to reply to Tate's words regarding their future, of what she would expect should they even contemplate marrying.

"Ava, this is Mr. Shelly the Runner I was telling you about. Mr. Shelly this is Miss Knight, my neighbor from Berkshire, and who came to my aid on the night of the fire at Cleremore."

The man bowed in her direction. "I'm pleased to meet you, Miss Knight."

Whatever Ava had pictured the Runner to look like it was certainly not what stood before her. This man was as tall as the duke and just as broad across the shoulders. His face, although not as pleasant as the duke's, in her opinion, he was certainly still very pleasing to the opposite sex with his dark, short locks and vibrant emerald eyes she'd not ever seen the like of before.

They all sat, and once settled, the duke said, "You have some information for us I understand."

Mr. Shelly threw her a curious glance and Ava smiled, knowing exactly what the poor man was thinking. What was a woman doing here in what should only be gentlemen's business?

"You may speak freely in front of Miss Knight. She knows of everything that has been occurring in Berkshire, and I do not hide anything from her."

Ava couldn't help the warm comforting feeling that engulfed her at the duke's words. He was such a very good man. She would be a fool indeed if she did not contemplate a future with him, but she would not if it meant sacrificing all that she'd worked so hard for.

But now was not the time to muse over what she wanted with the duke, or he in turn. Now was the time to find out if Lord Oakes was behind the awful attacks and if there was a possibility that he could be brought to justice.

"Of course Your Grace." The Runner reached into his pocket and pulled out a black notebook ruffling through a few of the pages. He stopped when he came to one page that Ava could see had points written upon the paper.

"The day you chased a gentleman in the woods and when he shot his flintlock in your direction, where unfortunately Miss Knight was injured after a fall." The Runner met her gaze. "I do hope you're feeling better, Miss Knight. I was quite distressed that the culprit had acted in such a way and toward a woman, no less."

Ava thanked him, knowing that if the culprit was indeed Lord Oakes that he was capable of worse deeds than shooting someone. Ava would rather go up against a gun any day, than be forced into a situation that she could not get out of or escape from. Just as Lord Oakes had tried to do to her.

"A farmer was working nearby and heard the shot. Within moments of the gun firing, the rider in question raced past where the farmer was standing. He does not believe he was seen. The culprit's bandana however by this time had slipped down to his neck, exposing his face. The farmer recognized this man as none other than Lord Oakes."

Ava met Tate's gaze and read the hope in his eyes that his lordship would soon be locked away and incapable of any more damage. To think she would not have worry about him ever again, be scared he would turn up at her door in the middle of the night and force himself upon her, finish what he started, sent hope soaring through her blood. He would be punished once and for all.

"I have men following Lord Oakes wherever his travels take him. We are watching where he goes, what business he deals in while in London and if he travels outside of the city, we'll know about it."

"This is encouraging news," the duke said. "Can we prove Lord Oakes was not in London on the day of the Cleremore fire or when Miss Knight and I were shot at?"

"We can," the Runner replied, "On both counts. We called at his lordship's London home and had a very insightful chat with his cook. The woman was quite willing to talk since we gifted her a crown. It also became known that his lordship is behind by a month on the servants' wages. The cook stated that although she didn't know where his lordship had gone, he had indeed traveled out of London. Of course, this is a commoner's word against a lord's, and that goes for the farmer as well. It is not enough evidence to prove his guilt, and if this did go to trial we would surely lose. But it is a start.'"

Ava frowned. This was all good information but it was not enough to bring Lord Oakes down. "What is your next step?"

The Runner grinned. "Lord Oakes will slip up at some stage and when he does, we'll be ready and waiting for him. In my experience, when they think they have outsmarted everyone, they do something that's not part of their original plan, and the knot they tie about themselves starts to unravel."

The duke nodded, seemingly pleased. "He's in London right now, and I've not been notified of any other fires from our home county. When we return to Berkshire, and if Lord Oakes too departs to his country estate, it will be interesting to see if any more incendiary attempts occur."

"I'm sure they will," Ava said. "He must enjoy inflicting such pain and suffering on others, and if I may impart an observation about his lordship."

Both the duke and the Runner glanced at her. "Please," Tate said, gesturing for her to speak her mind.

Ava cleared her throat, heat rising on her cheeks. "Mr. Shelly, I need you to know that Lord Oakes wished me to be his mistress some months ago. At the time he was courting a woman in town of substantial means and wanted to have a mistress near his country estate. I refused when I realized his intentions were not honorable."

"Ava, you do not need to tell…"

"Yes, I do," she said, interrupting Tate. "All of this needs to be known, at least to Mr. Shelly."

Tate sat back in his chair and Ava turned to the Runner. "It has not escaped my notice that the fires have been at properties that surround my own racing stables in Berkshire. I cannot help but think he's targeting those closest to me, my friends and neighbors, and leaving me till last."

The Runner's eyes widened with understanding and now having said her worries aloud, they did make sense. Lord Oakes had proven himself a selfish, mean human being. It would not surprise Ava if he wished to pay her back, torment her in this way before targeting her own home last.

"He would not dare," the duke said, murder in his tone.

The Runner looked between them before writing something in his note pad. "Your concerns are warranted, Miss Knight, and I shall have men stationed at your home to keep extra vigilance. Lord Oakes seems to have a sickness that is not curable," he said, blandly. "With an illness such as this, we do not know what he plans or when."

Ava could well believe that. "I suppose now we must be patient and wait, although it worries me where he'll strike next. If he's successful in his endeavors, what it will mean for those people? I know his cruel character. He is capable of inflicting pain on others and caring not at all that he has done so."

The Runner studied her a moment, seemingly thinking over her words. He folded his little black book closed and slipped it into his coat pocket. "There is no reason why someone will act out in such a way. Some people are inherently evil, wish to do harm to others for no other reason than it pleases them. We know Lord Oakes is in financial difficulties due to the woman he was courting having married someone else. Her father, you see, caught wind that his lordship had pockets to let and refused his suit. You turned down his advances, and those about him in Berkshire are prosperous, successful estates, nothing like his own."

Ava thought on the points. "And so, are you saying that you think he's targeting these estates, these families, simply because he's envious?"

The Runner shrugged. "People have murdered for less. I see no reason why Lord Oakes would not seek revenge for misdeeds concocted in his own feeble mind."

"This is disturbing," the duke said, thoughtfully. "I cannot deny that I shall be glad when Lord Oakes is behind bars or possibly sent to the colonies to never darken our doorsteps again."

"That is what we aim to do, Your Grace. It may take

some time but he will make an error, they all do at some point or another and when he does, we'll be ready."

Ava thought over the Runner's words. To wait was all well and good but Lord Oakes' desire to hurt people, his desire to see animals burn in their stables was not something she was willing to gamble with. Not something she was willing to allow Lord Oakes to do again. This time, no matter how many runners were following his lordship, they might be too late just as they had been too late to save Lord Morton's stable lad and horses only a few weeks ago.

"What do you think of the idea of saying something to Lord Oakes? Not that we have runners after him, simply hint that someone saw a gentleman riding off the day I was injured. Let his lordship's mind fester with the fear that someone had recognized him. If we were to say something such as that to him, it may scare him enough to stop him from starting any more fires ever again. I know we have to sit back and wait. I understand why you would do such a thing, but we risk so much with that plan. My stables, for instance, house horses that are worth hundreds of pounds. The prized thoroughbred Titan currently resides under my stables' roof. If we allow Lord Oakes to strike again, then we risk our livelihood, my staff and the horses' lives. What are your thoughts on that, Mr. Shelly? Do you think such a plan is worth a try?"

The Runner rubbed his jaw, pursing his lips in thought. "I see your dilemma and I understand the frustration behind it. We do risk a lot by waiting for him to strike again. But I think in this case we need to wait. My men have been instructed to hold off until the very last possible moment before they seize Lord Oakes, so if he does attempt to start a fire we will be there and we will stop him, but we need to catch him in the act. If he finds out that he is being watched or that you suspect him, he may bolt. The man is a coward at heart, and by running, well, we will never be able to prove his guilt if that happens."

Ava leaned back in her chair. She could understand his opinion but it still didn't make the prospect of letting him carry on any easier to stomach. "Very well," she conceded. "I will not say a word." Ava read the understanding in the duke's warm gaze and it gave her comfort. They would catch Lord Oakes and then they would be done with him. She would be done with him forever and maybe for the first time in an age, she would be able to breathe again.

"Very good," the duke said, "we're in agreement and that is settled. We will wait."

After discussing some miscellaneous items in relation to where the Runners will be housed between the duke and Miss Knight's estate, and who they were pretending to be so not to cause suspicion if Lord Oakes came upon them, the Runner bade them a good morning and left.

The duke, after bidding the man farewell, came back into the library, shutting the door behind him. Ava stood, knowing she too should leave. Even with the maid present, she was still risking her reputation by being there.

"I should be going too," she said, not moving. The duke reached out and took her hand, leaning over her gloved fingers and kissing them. His touch sent a frisson of awareness through her body and she squeezed his hand a little in return.

"Are you attending the Yorks' ball this evening? I understand that we're to attend with the viscountess."

The duke ushered her toward the door. "I'm attending now."

She chuckled and seeing the maid waiting patiently beside the door, she gestured for her to stand. "Until tonight then, Your Grace." Ava stopped at the library door threshold, drinking in the duke, as much as she could. She loved being alone with him. He was never the lofty peer of the realm with her. To her, he was simply Tate.

Whenever they were together her body never felt like her own. It shivered and craved his touch and she was powerless to stop it.

"Oh, how lovely," a cold, disinterested voice said from the stairs. "If it isn't Miss Knight. I thought my eyes were deceiving me last evening when I saw you at the Tinleys' ball. I did not think you were invited."

Ava took a calming breath and turned to smile at the dowager who leisurely strolled down the staircase toward them. Behind her stood a woman of striking beauty, all ethereal elegance and goddess-like with blonde flowing locks.

Ava curtsied and couldn't help but glance down at her own modest morning gown which was from last year's fashion plates. She steeled herself to ignore the word dowdy and plain that flittered through her mind whenever being around women who were fashionable, the *haut ton* and titled. She lifted her chin, determination straightening her spine.

She glanced at Tate, his face an awful shade of gray. He caught her looking at him and he shut his mouth with a snap, his lips thinning into an annoyed line. Toward her or his mother, Ava was uncertain, but she certainly hoped the latter.

"Tate, my dear, you remember Lady Clapham. She's my new companion and will be returning to Berkshire with me next week."

The woman dipped into a neat curtsy and something akin to jealousy shot through Ava at the sight of the striking beauty. She threw the duke an amused half smile, which only made her look prettier if that was even possible. For a moment Ava stared at them all, trying to place the name of her ladyship. Where had she heard it before?

Tate, seemingly remembering his manners, bowed slightly. "Welcome, Lady Clapham. I'm sure you will support my mother very well."

The dowager laughed. "Oh, indeed I do think she will."

Ava studied Lady Clapham and with sickening dread she remembered. She had been Tate's mistress. "Thank you again for the meeting, Your Grace. Good morning to you all." Ava collected her pelisse and bonnet from the footman who stood in the entrance hall, she didn't bother pulling it on, simply walked out as soon as the servant opened the door, her maid quickly following behind.

The way the duchess' companion looked at the duke was predatory. Were not companions supposed to be spinsters, women shy of nature, not interested in marriage or too old to catch the eye of a man? This Lady Clapham wasn't any of those things, but was perfect if the dowager had designs on her son keeping his distance from a woman of no rank and a businesswoman too.

"Miss Knight," the duke called, coming down the front stops of his home and meeting her at the door of the carriage. "I will see you tonight, will I not?" he asked, taking her hand and helping her up the steps of the vehicle.

She nodded, but wanting to go before he saw how jealous she was of the woman who would now live under his roof. She called out to the driver her directions.

To think Lady Clapham would have breakfast and dinner with Tate. Spend evenings before the fire in the parlor, playing games of cards and entertaining the dowager, like a little happily married couple. "I will see you then. Good day, Your Grace."

She didn't look at him as the carriage pulled away and she bit back the tears that threatened. This was why she was not made for this life. She was not a woman who played games, not like the dowager, or Lady Clapham who willingly took part in them too. This life was not who she was or wanted to be, something she needed to remember if she was to keep her head around Tate.

*T*ate stood on the footpath and watched the carriage rumble down the street until it turned a corner and went out of sight. He frowned knowing full well why Ava was upset with him, or more to the point, with his mother.

He turned on his heel and started back into his home, heading up to the first floor sitting room, where his mother had her private entertaining space. He found her with Lady Clapham, his former lover, no less, taking tea and smiling from ear to ear. No doubt their little coup that they had pulled off against Ava had gone very well.

"What," he said, pointing at Lady Clapham "is she doing here? And as your companion I might add. Are you mad, Mother? Should I call for the doctor and have you locked away at Bedlam before the day's end?"

The dowager narrowed her eyes, all amusement wiped at his words. "Lady Clapham is my companion and is dutifully keeping me company, amusing me as one's companion should. But if she also reminds you that you have a past, one that Miss Knight does not know about, well, all the better." His mother picked up her tea, taking a sip. "Whatever will Miss Knight say when I tell her that the woman who used to share your bed is now my companion?"

Tate didn't think his blood could boil any more fiercely than it had done when thinking about Lord Oakes, and yet, somehow his mother seemed to manage it very well. He fisted his hands at his side lest he try to strangle some sense into her. "You cannot make Lady Clapham your companion. Most of the gentlemen I know have been seeking out her attentions for months." Her ladyship gasped at his crassness, and Tate was sorry to offend her, but his mother and her schemes would help none of them. "No matter what you believe, Mother, Lady Clapham was not my mistress, she was simply a woman who warmed my bed for a time, a mutual agreement that is now over. If you do this, you will make yourself look ridiculous."

"I have every intention of doing so. I am the dowager duchess of Whitstone. No one would dare naysay me. Lady Clapham will be escorting me about Town and coming with me back to Berkshire. I, for one, am very excited about it all." His mother smiled, and yet only cold calculation was evident in her eyes.

"Why would you do such a thing? I always knew you were unloving, but I did not think you were so unkind to stoop to such levels. You ought to be ashamed of yourself." Tate glared at his parent.

His mother remained aloof and unmoved by his words. If he expected her to look even a little contrite, he was sadly mistaken. If anything she looked very well pleased with herself. "I am not, and I will not be. Lady Clapham is now working for me and we shall go about Town as much as I like. When I return to Berkshire, she too will come with me and we will make such a jolly party."

"You're not to return to Cleremore. I will send notice to the servants to have your things packed and moved over to the dower house. Your time as my parent who resides under my roof is over. As for the London home, you may remain here until you have organized alternate accommodation."

His mother shrugged, unfazed "Do what you wish, my dear. I shall see you at luncheon."

Tate stormed from the room. He fisted his hands to stop their shaking and fought the urge to strike out against the potted palm that sat against the passage wall.

Though he could not control his mother, he could control who lived in his houses. He started down the stairs. He would write to his steward at Cleremore at once, and have him pack everything up of his mother's and have it moved. He would not risk losing Ava again, no matter what underhanded schemes his parent came up with.

As for Lady Clapham, well he would talk to her about her conduct and what she thought she was up to, but without his mother being present. He thought he'd done the right thing by her, apparently she did not.

He shook his head, entering his library and locking the door behind him. Why, he'd even heard that she had a new lover already.

Tate didn't know that her ladyship's new patron was his mother. It wasn't to be borne.

CHAPTER 12

*L*ater that night, Tate stood beside his friend, Lord Duncannon, and watched as Ava danced with another gentleman of no importance. It was her fourth dance she'd had this evening, and upon his arrival not two hours before he was informed that her dance card was full and she would be unable to step out with him.

He took a sip of his wine, wondering how to explain to her that what she'd thought she'd seen at his house this morning was nothing to do with them. He might have found Lady Clapham attractive at one time, one would have to be blind not to. But how could he tell the woman who held his heart in the palm of her hand that she was the only woman who turned his head? The only woman to capture his heart and soul.

He'd not had a chance to talk to Lady Clapham as to why she was in cahoots with his mother, but he would. His bigger issue right now was how on earth was he to explain this situation to Ava without her being hurt by the truth.

"How is the hunt for the fire-starter coming along,

Tate? Has the Runner any leads as to who he thinks it is?" Lord Duncannon asked, sipping his wine.

Tate turned to his friend, having forgotten for a moment that he was even standing there. Duncannon was as tall as he was, but a little less wide across the shoulders. Even so, with his cutting jaw, blond locks and zest for life, he was often a favorite among the ladies.

"We do have a lead, and right at this moment the gentleman in question is talking to Lord York." They both glanced across the ballroom to where his nemesis stood. Anger spiked through Tate's blood and he restrained himself from storming across the few feet of parquetry floor that separated them to crack the bastard in the face. He watched him a moment, hating that he'd hurt Ava, terrorized and tried to rape her. Tate shook his head, thankful for Ava's maid who'd walked in and stopped him.

"Lord Oakes. You suspect him?" The shock in his friend's voice brought him out of his musings of how to torture the bastard if he ever had him alone.

"The day Miss Knight and I were shot at, although…"

"Wait. Stop," Duncannon said, clasping his upper arm. "You and Miss Knight, the very woman you wanted to marry all those years ago, were shot at? How do I not know of this?"

Tate shook his head. "Need I remind, you were not in London or England for that matter, at the time. How is Paris by the way? Still as decadent as ever and only too willing to put on a show for a wealthy viscount?"

His friend grinned. "Of course, but never mind that," he said, frowning. "Were either of you injured? What happened?"

"Look for yourself," Tate said, nodding in the direction Ava was still dancing with the Baron.

"That is Miss Knight?" Tate heard the appreciation in his friend's voice and chose to ignore it. Ava was very beautiful, even if she was unaware of the fact most of the time. And beauty, both in and out, which Ava had plenty of. It was no wonder she was quite sought after at balls and parties. The *ton* would miss her when she returned to Berkshire, even if Tate's mother did not.

"It is, yes."

Duncannon looked at him askance. "And she's dancing with someone else because?"

It was a question Tate had asked himself, but after Ava's hasty departure from his home earlier today, it wasn't hard to work out why she was avoiding him. She was angry and possibly hurt, but such emotions led to another thought. Ava cared for him, more than a friend and that in turn gave him hope.

"My mother has hired a new companion for herself. But the companion is Lady Clapham, a previous lover of mine."

"What!" The volume of Duncannon's statement had people turn in their direction, even Ava on the dance floor glanced over, catching Tate's eye before looking away.

"Shush, no one knows and she's only hired Lady Clapham so she can put a wedge between Ava, I mean Miss Knight, and myself."

"So you do care for her still. I thought as much when I saw you were not listening to me and your mind was elsewhere. While I did not know it was Miss Knight in particular that troubled you, I knew it had to be someone from the opposite sex."

Tate sighed, gesturing a footman over to deliver them some more wine. "It was not long after I returned to London. Miss Knight knows of some of the rumors that circulated Society about my shenanigans, but not all. Lady Clapham is one of them, but somehow my mother has found out and is setting out to cause trouble."

"You will have to put your mother in her place," Duncannon said, taking a glass of wine from the footman and smiling his thanks. "I care for the dowager of course, but she cannot rule your life as she is setting out to do. You're a grown man, Tate. You must let it be known you'll not have anyone in the family treat you with so little respect."

Tate clenched his jaw, knowing everything that Duncannon said was true. His mother had overstepped her bounds, and he would ensure she was settled in the dower house before he returned to Berkshire. But that did not mean she would not cause mischief between himself and Ava even located there.

He glanced to his left and inwardly swore. Lady Clapham strolled toward him, her best friend and one of the biggest gossips in the *ton* lodged firmly by her side. Feeling all the *ton*'s eyes on him, he looked back to where he'd seen Ava last on the ballroom and found her watching him with her group of friends.

"Talk of the devil," his friend said, bowing to the two ladies who joined them momentarily.

Tate had never wished to be anywhere else in the world than right at that moment. He did the right thing as was expected of a duke and bowed slightly to the ladies as they stopped before them. Lady Clapham smiled up at him, all sweetness that he knew was only skin deep. The woman had ice running through her veins if she had chosen to join forces with his mother.

He could only thank Providence that he'd learned this now, and had not offered for her last year when he was muddled and lovesick for a woman he'd not seen for a half a decade.

"Your Grace. Lord Duncannon." Both women curtsied and Tate fought not to glance back toward Ava to see if she was watching this all play out. Hell, he hoped she'd looked away, was once again dancing with another gentleman.

"Are you enjoying the ball?" Lord Duncannon asked, sipping his drink and seemingly enjoying Tate's awkwardness over the situation.

"We are," Lady Clapham smiled, sidling up closer to Tate. "We were just saying that the next dance is to be a waltz."

If that was an attempt by Lady Clapham to suggest that Tate to dance with her, she would be sorely disappointed. There was only one woman he wanted to dance with and that was Miss Knight. Unable not to, Tate sought her out once more and watched as the Marquess of Boothby bowed before her, taking her hand and placing it on his arm as he led her out onto the floor.

Tate drank down his wine, placing the glass on a side cabinet behind him. Damn the man. Anger spiked through his blood at the genuine smile that played on Ava's lips. Not to mention his lordship's hold was too low upon her back, and he was holding her far closer than he ought.

Bastard.

A hand clasped his upper arm, and he'd not known he'd taken a step toward the dance floor. "Let it go, Tate," his friend whispered. "She's only dancing. I think you have bigger issues at play right now than Miss Knight."

Duncannon's words doused his temper somewhat and he nodded, willing himself to trust in what he and Ava felt for one another, even if she were so very put out with him at present.

"Well, since I'm a widow and quite scandalous already, I shall have to take matters into my own hands. Will you dance with me, Your Grace?" Guests turned, some gasped at her ladyship's words. Tate narrowed his eyes, hating the game she played to his cost.

He clamped his jaw shut, before pulling his temper into line. To save her blushes and be a gentleman how could he not dance with her now? He held out his arm, smiling through gritted teeth. "Of course, Your Ladyship. Shall we?"

She took hold of him and lifting her chin, strolled beside him as he negotiated their place within the already waltzing couples. He did not enjoy the dance, his troubles only doubling with each moment Lady Clapham was in his arms. The music continued, people floated about them, swirling and laughing, and all he could see was Ava. Her attention engaged with the Marquess, not a moment spared for him.

How could she not leave one dance open for him? No one knew that he and Lady Clapham had been lovers, unless she'd been told more gossip than he was aware. The thought did little to calm his unease. It would certainly explain why she had left his London home so eagerly.

Damnation.

❧

*A*va fought not to look in the direction of Tate dancing with Lady Clapham, the very woman who had once been his lover and now resided under his roof. They made a striking pair as they waltzed about the room, the duke's steps effortless and perfect, making her ladyship look like she floated about like an angel.

The night had turned into one she'd sooner forget. With Lord Oakes' presence, it had started the night off on a downward spiral, but to see Tate dancing with a woman who was beyond beautiful, titled and liked by his Mother, left her less than pleased to be in Town witnessing it all.

When she'd heard that Tate had returned from America, his flouncing about in London hadn't affected her as much as it did now. She'd distanced herself from caring about what he was doing, and who he was associating with. Ignored it as best she could, or at least her heart's reaction to such news. Eventually she'd hardened, learned to rely on herself, look out for her workers and her horses and forget the duke who'd once claimed her heart.

But now, seeing him among his set, as the ladies fawned at his feet like some Greek god was unsettling. She took a calming breath, well it wasn't to be borne, and was certainly not something she would put up with. Not if the tears that threatened, each time she glanced in his way, was anything to go by.

Ava tried to concentrate on what the Marquess was talking to her about, but her mind was engaged elsewhere. Namely, the duke who now gazed down at Lady Clapham, deep in discussion. Thankfully the dance came to an end, and swinging her to a stop, she curtsied and thanked his lordship for the dance.

He bowed, and Ava didn't stay long enough to hear his final words, as she was already heading toward the retiring room. The last thing she needed was the *ton* to see her physically upset over a man that she herself had said she did not want to marry. Had not wanted that life for herself any longer, so why the upset? She shook the thought aside, angry at herself for being weak. For caring more than she'd wanted to.

Tate could dance with anyone he wished. He was free to court and marry and she'd made it as plain as day that she was happy with her life as it now stood. So why did the thought of him making someone else his wife bring out the worst of her character? The part that seethed made her stomach churn with dread, wonder what he was up to and with whom. The part of her that was jealous. So jealous that she could not act rationally or think clearly when that jealousy was baited, as it had been with the duke dancing with Lady Clapham.

"Ava," the duke called from behind her. She glanced over her shoulder, not altering her pace and certainly not willing to stop, lest she argue with him in public, where anyone could come upon them at any moment.

"Go back to the ball, Your Grace," she said, slipping into a room that had its door ajar and finding a vacant sitting room of some kind, the only light guiding her way from the bank of windows that ran the opposite length of it.

"Ava," he called again, following her into the room and closing the door behind him. The snip of the lock was loud in the space and she lifted her chin, meeting his gaze.

"Why did you lock the door? Actually, for that matter, why did you even follow me? Are you not supposed to escort your dance partner back to your Mother's side where she belongs?" She cringed at the envy that tinged her tone that would be evident to anyone listening.

He sighed, his shoulders slumping a little at her words. "I could ask the same of you. Why did the Marquess not take you back to your friends and the viscountess? You seemed to enjoy your dance very much, from what I could see."

Her temper soared and she growled, actually growled at the duke, before rounding on him. "Tell me what role Lady Clapham holds in your life? Your mother seems to like her very much and from her triumphant glances my way during your dance with her ladyship. I can only assume that she thinks you will be thrown together enough that you'll fall in love with her."

He frowned, shaking his head. "I do not care for Lady Clapham in any way other than a mutual acquaintance of my Mother's. If you must know she asked me to dance. I did not wish it."

Ava scoffed. "It did not look that way to me. In fact, you seemed quite happy to have her in your arms. I suppose I should not expect less since it's rumored you enjoyed having her in your arms very much last Season." Tate flinched but Ava stood by her words. She was not blind to how attractive Lady Clapham was, and why nearly every gentleman present sought her out.

"You're jealous." It was a statement of fact, and one Ava had to deny, even though it was as true as the sun rising in the east each morning.

"I am not jealous," she stated, the falsehood making her words come out thick and strained. "You may do as you please."

"Really?" he said, taking a step toward her. Ava stepped back. "Anything at all?" he asked again. He took another step.

She stopped moving knowing it was futile to try and outrun Tate. "Anything," her whispered word broke what restraint she held, and if Tate thought that it would be he who would decide what happened next, Ava would lay that thought to rest.

She closed the space between them, reached up and took his lips in a searing kiss. The moment they touched a wave of rightness swamped her and she knew this was where she wanted to be. Not dancing with anyone else, or alone in Berkshire training horses, but in the arms of the boy whom she'd always loved, had lost and found once again as a grown man.

His arms wrapped about her and he hoisted her up against him, his lips as insistent as her own. She could sense the desperation and need in each stroke of his tongue, of his hands against her back that couldn't seem to get her as close as he'd like.

Not that there was very much distance between them. For Ava could feel every line, every curvature of his body, including what strained against her belly and made her all shivery inside.

He walked her backwards until the settee hit the back of her knees. But not stopping there, they collapsed onto the cushioned seat, Tate's weight pinning her to the chair. Their kiss didn't stop, and nor did she halt Tate when his hand slid down her leg to lift the hem of her gown.

Cool air kissed her ankle, her calf and finally her thigh. Tate lifted himself a little, adjusting to lie fully between her legs and liquid heat swamped her core. Being here with Tate in such a way did not bring forth the fear she thought it would. To be held down beneath him with their intentions clear, she thought that maybe panic would assail her, but it did not. Not with Tate. Delicious desire and never-ending need that only he could sate, was all she felt and longed for.

He glanced down at her, his breathing ragged, but even

so Ava trusted that should she say stop, he would do as she asked.

"Is this what you want, Ava? You know, I would never do anything that you did not desire."

She reached up, running a hand over his cheek, the faintest growth of stubble prickling her palm. His dark hair flopped over his forehead giving him a wicked air, and she sighed, her heart full with the affection that she felt for the man before her.

"I don't want you to stop."

He kissed her again, deep and sure and she lost herself within his arms. Let herself go to enjoy all that he could give her tonight. He sat back and reached beneath her gown, sliding her drawers out of the way. Tate's eyes darkened and Ava shivered as the soft cotton slid over her legs, leaving only her stockings and silk slippers on.

Not willing to deny herself him any longer, Ava reached across and clasped his breeches. With fingers that shook, either from nervousness or expectation, she wasn't sure. Ava flicked the buttons open wanting this for them, to lie in his arms and be the woman who brought forth all the desire and need she could read in his eyes, in his touch and every kiss.

Flipping the final button open on his breeches, Ava reached inside and clasped his hard member. She sucked in a breath at the softness of the skin that encased steel. His eyes met hers, dark and swirling with an emotion that left her heady and drunk on expectation. That is was her who made Tate react so. That it was her he desired and no one else.

Not the beautiful Lady Clapham or any other woman he'd been linked with over the past five years, but her.

"Kiss me," she asked.

She need not ask again. Tate took her lips in a searing kiss and Ava wrapped her legs about his hips, wanting him with a craving she'd never felt before. His sex slid against hers, teasing and torturous. She moaned as warmth rushed between her thighs. Tate reached down between them to guide himself into her.

"You're ready for me," he growled against her lips. "Tell me you're sure."

"Mmmm," she said, wiggling a little to try and get him to finish what they'd started. "I want this." She could not wait too much longer. She'd already waited years to have him just so, his delaying tactics, his teasing was not warranted. "Don't make me beg, Tate," she said, pushing against him and eliciting a need to pulsate through her abdomen.

"Oh, I won't make you wait at all."

~

*T*ate ran his fingers over the cleft of her cunny, soft and wet and ready for him to make her his own. She undulated against his hand and his cock twitched, hard as stone and dripping with his own need to have her.

Their location was not ideal, and vaguely Tate could remember snipping the lock on the door, but nothing and no one would move him from where he was right now. He'd waited so long to have Ava. He had dreamed of them being together in such a way.

She glanced up at him, her eyes dark with unsated need and trust and his heart gave a thump in his chest. How he adored her. She was everything he wished for in a wife, a lover and friend and there was no chance in hell that he'd let her go now that he had her back.

After today, after they gave themselves to each other in this way, he would marry her. Love her and ensure that Miss Ava Knight became the next Duchess of Whitstone.

"You're so wet," he said, slipping a finger into her hot core. He groaned when she tightened her inner muscles about his fingers, pulling on him, drawing him in.

"I am," she gasped, clutching at his shoulders while he pushed a little further inside. "I want you, Tate. I want you so much."

Unable to wait a moment longer, he pulled out, hoisted her legs higher on his hips and guided himself into her.

She lay back, closing her eyes and sighed her pleasure that only made his cock harder. There was little resistance, and he was thankful for it, not wanting to mar this time with anything painful that could tarnish her memory. Their joining was something to celebrate and relish and he would make it everything she'd ever hoped.

"Oh, Tate," she sighed, leaning up to kiss him. "You feel so good, so right."

Tate pulled out a little before thrusting forward and her words had never been more true. Hell, this did feel right and good and everything else he could think of. They moved into a synchronized rhythm and he fought not to lose himself before she found pleasure. He wanted to see her shatter in his arms, to clench and spasm about his cock that would pull himself into climax.

Their movements became more frantic and Ava's breathy moans and sighs of pleasure were too much. He would spill himself if he did not do something to bring Ava to climax and soon.

Tate pulled out and kneeled between her legs, pushing her knees apart.

"What are you doing?" she asked breathlessly, trying to close her legs a little. He clasped her hands and placed them behind her head. "Hold the settee's arm rest. I want to taste you."

"Taste me? Whatever do you mean?"

He didn't answer, merely leaned down between her legs and licked Ava from core to clit. Her sweet musky scent made him moan, and licking her again he settled to tease the little nubbin that begged for release.

"Oh, my," she gasped.

Oh, yes... Tate looked up to see her place her hand across her mouth. He slid his tongue back and forth over her sex, loving the taste of her, that without guidance she undulated against his lips, seeking release. He didn't let up his assault on her sex, wanting to give her pleasure before he made love to her. She gasped his name and letting go of the settee's arm rest, spiked her fingers through his hair, holding him against her.

Tate felt the contractions against his fingers and smiled, kissing her fully, enjoying the moment as she climaxed against his mouth.

When he'd followed Ava into the corridor he had never dreamed this is where they would end up, but by God, he was thankful they had. The last thing he wanted was for them to be at odds over other people's reactions or plans.

He kissed her mons before coming up to settle between her legs once more. She opened for him, her eyes half closed and sleepy with satisfaction.

Tate guided himself into her heat, and she merely closed her eyes, sighing. "Are you well, my darling," he asked, lifting her chin with his finger so she would look at him. He slowly pumped into her, wanting to drag out his time with her as much as possible.

She met his gaze and smiled dreamily. "Oh yes, I'm more than well. Don't stop," she said, wrapping her arms about his shoulders and lifting her legs to sit about his back.

Her acceptance of him, her willingness broke what little control he had and he thrust into her, wanting to make her his and his alone.

She gasped, pulling him down for a flagrant kiss.

He kissed her deep, his tongue mimicking his strokes and within a few minutes he wanted to lose himself within her. But not yet, it was too soon. He had to hold off a little longer.

She reached down with one hand, clasping the cheek of his ass and pulled him deeper. With a tilt of her hips Tate sheathed himself fully and his restraint fractured. He thrust into her, once, twice, three times and came with such force that he forgot their location and called out her name.

Ava gasped, moaning his in turn and the sound of her enjoyment was a match to his flame. She was as perfect for him as the day he'd asked her to marry him all those years ago. He'd wanted nothing more than to bundle her up, take her home and keep her in his bed and life for forever and a day.

He collapsed to the side of her on the settee, pulling her to lie in the crook of his arm. The clock on the mantle clicked, marking the late hour of one in the morning. "I do not ever wish to move. I would be quite content to stay here with you forever if I could."

Ava ran her hand over his chest, playing with the buttons on his waistcoat that he'd not even removed in their haste to have one another. "And I too, alas, we cannot. We must return to the ball before we're missed."

Tate sighed, not wanting to do anything. "If I agree to take you back to the ball, will you dance with me?" He turned to meet her gaze. "Do I warrant a place on your dance card now?"

She grinned, raising her brow. "I think you do," she said, turning to look up at the ceiling and growing serious of a sudden. "If you want to know the truth for my displeasure, I know your history with Lady Clapham and I couldn't stand it. A woman who is titled, beautiful and elegant, of your social sphere. Well, I'm not fool enough not to know I was jealous."

He turned her face to look at him, beseeching her to believe his words. "I'm not looking at Lady Clapham to be my wife." *I want you as my wife, to be by my side always.* He didn't say the words, not yet at least, but he would. Everything that lay between them needed to be discussed and soon. "She is merely in the dowager's employ and nothing more."

When it came to Ava, there was no one who occupied his heart as much as she did. She had always been the one. A realization he'd come to know the moment she confronted him at his stables after five years of not seeing her.

"When we return to Berkshire we will discuss what this all means. What we want." He wanted her. As his wife, his confidant and partner. Nothing else would do.

She smiled, leaning up to kiss him quickly. "I think that would be best."

CHAPTER 13

I realized today that I have moved on in my life. That although marriage is not something that I desire any longer, know that I'm happy.

— An Excerpt from a letter from Miss Ava Knight to the Duke of Whitstone

The following morning Ava woke late and rolled over on her mattress to stare out of the window of her room. She'd heard a maid come in earlier and open the blinds, carrying in some fresh water and wash cloths, but Ava had fallen back to sleep.

The ball the previous evening had turned out much better than Ava had thought it would. Certainly after being a jealous little swine over Lady Clapham and all but storming out of the duke's home earlier that morning, she'd not thought he would explain her ladyship's situation.

How wrong she'd been. Not that it changed much

about their predicament, but it did make her feel some-what better knowing his attachment to the lady was over. Still, she thought the best course for her was to keep her independence. The duke was so very revered within Soci-ety, people looked up to him, he was kind and a lot was expected of him. The role of his wife would be a massive undertaking, and Ava wasn't convinced she wanted it.

One thing she was sure of however was that she wanted Tate. The fire that burned, licked and charred their resolve whenever they were near one another could not be ignored. But there was another option they'd not contemplated, that of them becoming lovers.

Making what had occurred at Lord York's ball a permanent arrangement between them.

No marriage, no contracts, no expectations, simply time together, enjoyment and pleasure.

Nerves fluttered in her belly at the memory of what they'd done in that private room. Ava grinned, biting her bottom lip. She wanted to do it again and soon.

She pushed back her bedding and went about her morning routine before dressing in a light blue morning gown. Before she headed back to Berkshire she'd gone into Hatchards and ordered some books on horse breeding and lineage and they were supposed to be in by today. She would call in the bookstore before heading over to Hyde Park to meet with Hallie and Willow.

With the viscountess living in Mayfair it was only a short walk to Hatchards, and at the early hour when most households would still be abed after a late night at balls and parties about London, Ava had little trouble making it to the store within reasonable time.

The little bell above the door chimed as she entered, and saying hello to the clerk behind the desk, she walked about to see if there were any other books she would like. The comforting scent of leather and polish permeated the air, the quiet, hushed tones of other booklovers in the store as they walked about made her smile.

For a time, Ava lost herself within the rows of books, the variety on offer, before one book in particular caught her eye. Opening the tome, she gasped, shutting it with a snap.

Looking about Ava checked that she was alone, and seeing that she was so, opened it again to see images of men and women, sometimes more than two in all sorts of bed play.

She stared as one image in particular that showed a woman lying in the opposite direction to her lover and Ava couldn't imagine such a way was even possible. How would that even work?

She shut the book, placing it back and determined to read it further when she was in next. Right now if she did not leave she would be late meeting her friends in the park.

It didn't take her long to pick up her books, and thanking the clerk, she walked out onto Piccadilly, turning toward Hyde Park and running head on into a wall of muscle that was standing before her.

For a moment Ava thought it might be Tate, until she looked up and all hopes for such a reunion was dashed.

"Miss Knight. How opportune it is to meet you here. Are you in a rush to be somewhere else by chance?"

The answer was a resounding yes. Yes, she was in a rush to meet her friends, but even more so now she was in a rush to get away from him.

"Excuse me," she said, moving past Lord Oakes. She started when he clasped her hand and wrapped it about his arm, joining her on her walk to Hyde Park.

Panic tore through her at being alone with him again. She'd sworn after the day he tried to assault her that she'd never be alone with anyone she did not trust and she certainly did not trust Lord Oakes by any means.

"So," he said, all joviality. "Where are we off to in such a rush? Are you going to meet the Duke of Whitstone again, or someone else?" He grinned down at her and his attempt to be amusing came off as nothing but a sneer.

Never did Ava think she could loathe someone as much as she hated the lord beside her, but alas, here she was with the one man she'd prefer to be dead than be with alive.

"If you must know I'm meeting my friends, Miss Evans and Miss Perry in Hyde Park. Not that it's any of your business." She tried to pull her hand free to no avail.

He tsked tsked her, smiling at a passer-by as if their little tête-à-tête was normal and commonplace. "Come now, Miss Knight. We know each other on a personal level. Do not be cold with me. There was a time you were all too willing and quite hot to touch."

She wrenched her arm free, rounding on him and bedamned where they were. "I was never willing. And you may think whatever you like, but if you come near me again, I will make you pay." She wasn't sure how she would accomplish this, but she would, even if that meant swallowing her pride and asking Tate to help her with his lordship. Not an option she relished since she was so very determined to keep her independence, but still, sometimes a man was required to pull other men back into line.

Lord Oakes lifted his hand and ran his finger over the wrist she injured. Very few people knew of her being wounded and why her horse had reared, causing her to fall. So how did Lord Oakes know of such a thing unless...

She narrowed her eyes and he grinned before pushing

against her healed wound harder than one ought and she gasped, stepping away.

"I do apologize, Miss Knight. Are you sore there?"

She stared at him a moment, not believing he would be so brazen. "You ought to know, Lord Oakes," she said, seeing if he understood her words.

His eyes widened and then, throwing his head back he laughed as if she'd said something extremely amusing. People walking down Piccadilly glanced in their direction but continued on without comment. "Oh, you're a true beauty. I know now why I wanted you so much, if only to try and tame the little beast that rumbles in your soul."

"You have no soul," she said without thought. "So it would only make sense for you to try and take it from someone else." His admittance of being there that day was an odd thing to do. He may not have said the actual words, but he all but admitted to knowing of her injury and how it came about. Lord Oakes was the fire-starter, of that she had no doubt, but still, it was her word against his lordship, a female voice against that of a man's. A powerful man even if his pockets were to let by all accounts.

"You cannot prove a thing, my dear, beautiful Miss Knight. And your word against my own is moot, worthless, so if I were you, I would not try and sully my name. Even so, looking at you now, knowing what a fine piece of flesh you are, it does make me hard with want of you."

She recoiled, starting toward the park. He caught up to her, keeping to her quickened pace. "Does the duke know of our rendezvous? Does he know how you moaned my name that day in your parlor when I stroked your cunny?"

Tears pooled in her eyes and she blinked them away. "Leave, you've said enough and I will not listen to you a moment longer."

"Oh, but you will listen, you little whore." He pulled her to a stop, his grip on her upper arm painful, yet she refused to cringe, to buckle under his assault.

"I saw you last night with the duke. I saw everything…" he smirked. "I want you in my bed. I think I've waited long enough to have you."

A tremor ran through her, leaving her cold. She swallowed, looking about and thankfully seeing that the people on the street were paying them little mind. "You will never have me," she whispered fiercely.

"If you do not comply," he continued, "I will ruin your little horseracing business and breeding program and you'll be left with nothing, no income, no customers, and no duke," he whispered sadistically against her ear. "How sad you will be then. As sad as you were when the duke was abroad and you returned home to Berkshire. Or when he finally returned to England and decided to remain in London, fucking who knows how many women. But," he shrugged, "it is the way of my society. Lords take lovers and wives wait at home."

She flinched, hating the idea of such a marriage. Hating the thought of Tate making love to anyone else but herself. "You may threaten me with whatever you choose. I will not do what you ask." Her mind reeled, wanting to leave, to get away from Lord Oakes.

He chuckled, letting go of her arm. "We shall see, Miss Knight. Good day to you," he said, bowing before walking off in the opposite direction.

Ava turned for the park, not slowing her quickened pace until she spied Hallie and Willow. Her friends had always been a place of comfort and safety and right at this moment she needed them more than ever.

Willow waved to her as she came nearer to them, and

Ava schooled her features to hide the turmoil that twisted and turned within her.

"Ava, we're so glad you're here. We're discussing the ball and the Marquess of Boothby's home. You know the gentleman, you danced with him at the Yorks' ball. It's this evening, and we're deciding on what to wear. We thought we may all dress in matching pastel colors so to look like a set. What do you think of our idea?"

Ava nodded, smiling and mumbling her agreement while her mind whirled with what to do. Could she tell the duke of Lord Oakes' threat? If she did tell Tate what had transpired today, he would call him out. Lord Oakes had already proven himself as a man who didn't shy away from firing upon innocent people. The thought of losing Tate in such a way made bile rise in her throat.

No, she would keep this to herself, go back to Berkshire and deal with Lord Oakes in the country, away from the prying eyes of the *ton* if she could manage it. He would trip up soon enough in all his nefarious dealings and threats, and then the law would take care of him for them all.

~

*U*pon her return home, Ava could hardly remember how the past hour had gone by, what she and her friends had discussed or whom they had run into. All she knew was that she wanted to be alone, away from all the noise of London and back in Berkshire.

"If you'll excuse me, I think I'll lie down for a time. I have a sudden headache."

"Are you well?" Hallie asked, taking her hand and halting her steps in the foyer of the viscountess' home.

"I think not, unfortunately. I do believe that my

196

megrim will stop me from attending the ball this evening. I hope you don't mind," she said and meaning it. Above all else she wanted to see Tate again. Just being in his presence would calm her nerves, but she could not face the *ton*. Lord Oakes undoubtedly would be there. Not tonight.

"Of course, my dear," Willow said, coming over to her after she handed her shawl and bonnet to a waiting footman. "I shall have a tisane made and sent up to you directly."

"Thank you," Ava said, undoing her bonnet and starting up the stairs. "That is very kind of you."

~

*T*ate stood beside Lord Duncannon and his gut churned at the absence of Ava at the ball. Where was she? Her friends were here and were dancing and conversing happily, but Ava was not.

He bided his time, and seeing them partake in a glass of punch between sets, strolled over to them. "Good evening, Miss Evans, Miss Perry. I hope you're enjoying the night's festivities?" His banal conversation bored even him, but he would do the pretty so to ensure if Ava was well.

"We are thank you Your Grace."

They stared at him with knowing, amused visages and yet ventured nothing further. He couldn't outright ask about Ava, but dear God, he wished he could. These social rules and expectations really were a bore at times.

"Have you attended the marquess' ball before or is this your first time?"

Miss Evans considered him with a studied air before she said, "This is my first time in London for some years. As you know I attended school in France with Miss Knight and Miss Perry. Miss Perry attended this ball last year, as Viscountess Vance is her aunt."

Finally, Tate had his opening to enquire about Ava. "And Miss Knight, is she not here this evening with you? I thought she was a guest also of the viscountess?"

Miss Evans raised her brow, her lips twitching. "Alas no Your Grace, she's indisposed at home this evening unfortunately."

He stepped toward them, about to enquire further and then thought better of it. "Well, that is a shame. I do hope she's better by tomorrow."

"Oh, so do we," Miss Perry said. "We have a night at Vauxhall Gardens planned and we'd sorely be disappointed if Ava is unable to attend."

"You're attending the masquerade?" Tate had thought it was an event normally for those of low morals and pastimes that took place more on their backs than on socializing with the *ton* looking for a little distraction.

Miss Evans shushed her friend, catching her gaze. "I do apologize, Your Grace. My friend is mistaken. We're not attending Vauxhall at all. We're staying in tomorrow night."

Tate watched the play between friends and understood that Miss Perry had misspoken. He bit back a smile at her lapse and schooled his features. "I hope Miss Knight is not so very ill. I would so hate for her to miss out on the pleasure gardens."

Miss Perry chuckled. "It is merely a headache, Your Grace, but I misspoke before. We're at home tomorrow evening."

"And are you attending any more balls this evening? Or is Lord Boothby's ball enough to satisfy you both."

Their cheeks blossomed into a light shade of pink,

making them as pretty as the women about them who stood adorned with diamonds and silks.

"Tonight we have two other balls to attend after this one, Your Grace. The viscountess' good friend Lady Southerton is expecting us next and has promised some fireworks for her guests.

"That sounds most exciting." Tate bowed. "I wish you an enjoyable evening. Please send my regards to Miss Knight when you see her next."

Tate turned on his heel, heading toward the ballroom doors. He made a hasty farewell to Lord Duncannon before calling for his carriage. The journey to Berkley square was quick and telling his driver to park in the mews, he started for the front door, knocking twice before a footman bid him entry.

He handed his card to the butler. "Please have Miss Knight attend me in the library at once."

The butler studied his card only a moment before he guided Tate toward a room at the front of the house. "This way Your Grace. I shall see if Miss Knight is available, she was unwell this afternoon."

"Your Grace?" A female voice said from atop the stairs. He glanced up and his apprehension at hearing of her illness abated a little at seeing her again.

"Miss Knight. I do apologize for this intrusion. I have news from Berkshire that I thought you might be interested in hearing. Being a fellow land owner as you are," he lied. Willing to say anything to have her come downstairs to talk to him.

"Thank you, John. I shall see the duke in the library. We're not to be disturbed."

The servant bowed and left them. Tate waited at the base of the stairs for Ava before he escorted her into the library. He went ahead as Ava closed the door behind them, and grinned at the snip of the lock that sounded loud in the room. "What are you doing here, Tate? If you're caught by the viscountess we'll both be ruined."

"I noticed your absence at the ball this evening and when your friends mentioned a megrim, I was concerned. I could not rest before I saw for myself that you were well."

Ava joined him before the fire. "You were worried about me?"

He smiled, pulling her against him and holding her close. "You know I would be."

She clutched him back and looking up, Tate's heart did a little thump in his chest. She was so beautiful in her day gown, no ornaments or rouge upon her cheeks that a lot of the women of the *ton* were so fond of. Ava looked like a woman who'd been enjoying a night at home, reading or simply relaxing in her room. Her long dark locks sat about her shoulders and he itched to run his hand through them, feel their softness and sweet scent.

"Are you feeling better?" he asked, pushing a lock of her hair behind her ear.

She nodded. "I never had a headache, I wanted a night to myself, but I'm happy to see you."

Tate liked hearing such words. He liked seeing her as well. Could imagine many nights such as these, together, alone where they could talk, simply enjoy each other's company, just as they had as children.

"You said you had something to tell me about Berkshire and Lord Oakes?"

He grinned. "I don't have anything to impart. I simply wanted to see you again."

"You did?"

"I did," he said.

Her sweet voice did odd things in his chest. He leaned down and kissed her, took her lips and tried to import with all his heart how much she meant to him. Ava went willingly into his arms, her fingers slid over his shoulders to wrap about his neck. Her breasts pushed against his chest, her pliant, womanly curves drawing him in as they always did.

Tate leaned down and swooped her into his arms, picking her up and carrying her to a nearby chair. He sat, placing her onto his lap so she straddled him. He kissed her hard, licking her bottom lip, tracing the sweep of her mouth, unable to get enough of her. So soft and willing and the word *mine* reverberated about in his head. She opened for him and he deepened the kiss. His tongue slid against hers, and he moaned, fire igniting his blood.

Ava broke from the kiss, her breathing as ragged as his and for a moment they stared at one another. Emotions crashed through him watching her wide brown eyes stare at him in wonder, realizing that they affected each other the same. It should not surprise either of them it had always been like this. The first time they'd kissed under a large oak tree, they had both come away from that embrace forever changed, linked by some invisible tie that, even as young as Tate had been at that time, he'd known. She was meant to be his, forever.

He ran his thumbs across her cheeks, holding her face before him. Ava shuffled on his lap, placing her heat hard upon his. She sighed, rocking against him, her hot core tempting him to rip open the front of his breeches, and seal them together.

Tate shook with his denial to do exactly what they so obviously wanted. Somewhere in the recesses of his mind he reminded himself where he was. That he'd entered the room, and had not locked the door. An oversight on his behalf.

"I should go. If the viscountess comes home there will be hell to pay," he said between kisses. "I do not want trouble for you." Not that he would not marry Ava tomorrow, but she did not need the *ton* to shun and talk about her if they did find out about their tryst. His marriage to Ava would be because they wished it to be so, not because the *ton* thought he'd ruined her in some way and was forced into the union.

"I don't want you to go," she protested, in a tremulous voice. Taking his hand, she pushed it down to lie against her sex. Her wet cunny greeted him and he hardened to steel. He would not deny her, them both, not when she wanted this as much as he. Tate ran his fingers along her core, eliciting a sweet gasp from her lips. She pressed down on his hand, her eyes turning deep amber with flecks of fire in them.

"I want you, Tate!" She kissed him hard. "You make me crave you so much."

Tate moaned as her hand slid down his abdomen, taking pains to caress the contours of his stomach before delving further and wrapping itself around his engorged cock. "You make me want you too," he rasped, breathless.

Her fingers made quick work of the buttons on his breeches and then she was touching him, sliding her clever hand about his cock, a steady stroke that sent stars to flicker behind his eyes.

Ava shuffled closer and kissed him. "I saw in a book a position like we are now. Do you...do you think," she continued, "that such a position may be possible for us?"

What types of books was she reading? He wanted to know more. He left that question for another time, too distracted with her movements upon his lap. If he were at all a gentleman he would give her some days' grace before they made love again, but such an option was impossible when her penetrating stare all but begged him to fulfill her.

And he'd do exactly as she asked.

"You only need to ask." He grinned and reached between them, gathering her gown and hoisting it about her waist. She lifted herself a little, helping him with his endeavor. Their movements were quick and desperate. The need to have her, fuck her and lay claim to the woman in his arms was too much. He positioned himself at her entrance, catching her sultry gaze.

Tate thrust hard into her as she slid down over his length. Her tight core wrapped about him and he sucked in a breath at the sheer exquisiteness of having her again. They rocked together, her arms circling his neck, her fingers clawing into the skin on his back. He pumped hard and deep, wanting her to shatter in his arms, to come apart with him.

She was his, now and forever, just as he was hers. How could it not be so when each time they came together it was simply right? After all the years apart, still, they had found each other again.

Ava pushed him against the back of the seat, her hands clasping the chair. Tate reveled in watching her take control, finding her own pace to take pleasure from him. She was utterly marvelous, and he clamped down his need to spill inside of her. He reached between them, sliding his fingers against the little nubbin at her core. A half gasp, half moan escaped her lips and he gasped.

"Come for me," he begged, so close that temptation licked his every thrust.

Her movements became desperate, and he clasped her

hips, guiding her deeper, harder each time she came down upon him. Her fingers clasped his nape, sliding up into his hair and he knew she was close. Her eyes fluttered shut, the slightest perspiration on her upper lip that he ached to lick.

"Oh, Tate." She threw her head back as spasm after spasm clenched about his cock, pulling him along into climax. Tate came hard, following her into bliss where he wanted nothing more than to do it again. He fought to catch his breath, to come back to reality after taking his fill. She slumped against his chest, her breathing warm upon his shoulder. She turned her head, kissing his neck and he shivered with renewed need.

He would never tire of the woman in his arms.

"However are we going to stop?" she giggled and he wrapped his arms about her, holding her close.

He kissed her forehead, catching her gaze. "I have no idea," he said, truthfully. And he did not, but nor did he wish to.

"I should feign a megrim more often, if you're my remedy."

Minx! He chuckled, holding her still and with little desire to move her from his lap. "It is only fair that I'm your cure, for you've always been mine."

CHAPTER 14

*S*ome days' later Tate rode hard on the road out of London heading toward Berkshire. He'd finished up his work with his steward earlier than he had anticipated and with any luck he would catch up with Ava's coach.

He smiled at the thought of her. How much he missed her when they were apart.

The Ugly Swan Inn came into view a little way ahead, and he slowed his horse's pace as he started through the outskirts of the small village. People milled about the town going about their business. The Inn was busy with an array of carriages and people unloading and loading the equipages.

Halting in the Inn yard, a young stable lad ran out, and getting down, Tate handed the boy a shilling. "Tell me lad, is a Miss Ava Knight and her party still here or have they moved on?"

The young boy's eyes widened and nodding excitingly, he said, "Aye, they're still here, my lord. They're inside this past hour and have taken rooms so me pa says."

"Thank you," Tate said, dismissing the boy and his use of my lord instead of your grace.

He opened the Inn's front door and entered what looked to be the front tavern area of the establishment. It was filled to the brim with travelers and local folk from the looks of their dusty, crinkled and workworn clothing. Tate walked up to the counter and slid a sovereign across the bar. "I need a room for the night. I also need to know where Miss Knight is located within your premises so I may make my presence known."

The barman, a rotund, graying sort of man raised his brow, crossing his arms across his belly. "And who may you be?" he asked. Tate had to give him credit for asking instead of telling anyone of Ava's whereabouts when money was offered.

"I am the Duke of Whitstone."

The barman's eyes widened and he straightened, attempting to bow to him. "The party that ye enquire about is currently having a repast in the front private parlor, Your Grace. I will have my best chamber prepared for ye at once. 'Tis the first door on the left as ye go upstairs."

"Thank you," Tate said, starting for the room.

He knocked twice and opened the door to find Ava alone at the table. She sat in the sunlight with the Times paper open before her. She looked up and surprise registered on her face, before she placed the paper down and started toward him.

"Tate, whatever are you doing here?"

He shut the door and caught her up in his arms. "Two days was too long."

She smiled and kissed him and he took her lips, drank

from them as if she were his last hope of quenching his thirst.

Ava melted against his chest and the feel of her breasts, her nipples hardened peaks through her soft cotton traveling gown made his blood race in his veins. He kissed her deep and long, hoisted her up against his person and left them both breathless.

"Damn, I want you," he gasped through the kiss.

"Are you staying the night?" she asked him in turn.

He'd stay forever if only she'd allow. "I have a room." He held her close, not wanting to let her go. "Would you care to join me?"

She threw him a wicked look that sent his blood to boil. "I will have to tell Hallie what I'm doing or she'll worry. But I'm sure she won't mind."

The door opened and in walked her friend as if by saying her name aloud Ava had summoned her. She started seeing the duke holding her friend in a most inappropriate way. She entered quickly, before closing the door just as fast before anyone saw them.

Tate gently set Ava away from him and smiled at the light blush that stole over her cheeks. Ava went to sit back at the table and Hallie joined her not saying a word. Tate sat also, and picking up the pot of tea he poured himself a cup.

Hallie glanced back and forth between them, before sighing. "What are you two doing? You're not married or engaged and yet I walk in here, in the middle of a busy country inn and find you both in each other's arms." Miss Evans reached for the bread and cheese, placing a good portion on her plate when neither of them ventured to answer. "Oh, and by the way, the dowager duchess has just arrived."

"What?" Both he and Ava said in unison. Tate stood and walked to the window, looking out onto the Inn yard. He inwardly swore at the sight of his mother and Lady Clapham organizing help with their luggage, a bevy of servants doing the duchess' bidding.

He looked down at Ava just as she caught his eye and he read the wariness that entered them. "I'm sorry. I didn't know that my mother was traveling home today."

She clasped his arm, squeezing it a little. "You have nothing to apologize for, Tate."

His mother entered the inn, and within a moment there was a quick knock on the parlor door before she walked in with her companion. His mother took in the room and the occupants and gave a dismissive sniff.

"Tate, my dear, why didn't you tell me that you were leaving for Berkshire today, I would've ensured there was room for you in the equipage." His mother sat at the table after the servant who opened the door for them pulled out a chair for her grace.

"I did not know you were traveling for one. Second, I have my horse."

Lady Clapham caught Tate's eye and smiled up at him all but ignoring Ava and Miss Evans who sat at the table across from them.

"Will you escort us to Berkshire in the morning, Your Grace? With the man terrorizing the county lighting fires, or so I heard, it would settle both mine and your Mother's nerves if we had a protector at our side."

Miss Evans smiled and Tate understood very well as to why. Lady Clapham's tone oozed sin, even with his mother's presence, and Tate didn't miss that Ava's hands had fisted about the paper she was holding.

"Of course, I shall escort you to the dower house,

Mother. I had word only yesterday that it is ready for your arrival, fully staffed just as you like things. And if I may be so bold, Miss Knight, Miss Evans, I can escort you also if you'd like to travel with us."

Ava looked between him and the dowager. His mother's mouth had tightened up to a small pucker of distaste and it was not hard to know what she thought of the idea.

"We would like that, Your Grace," Miss Evans answered when Ava remained quiet.

"If you'll excuse us, Your Graces, Lady Clapham, we've traveled a long way today and I think I'll rest before dinner."

Tate moved out of the way to allow Ava to move past him. He reached down and slid his hand against her fingers as she walked past. She didn't respond, merely left him alone with his vexing parent.

He ground his teeth for the forthcoming discussion to be had. Damn he was sick of his mother's interfering, rude ways. He'd warned her to keep her tongue in check, and yet still, she persisted to be insolent.

"I see Miss Knight is still chasing your coat tails, Tate dear. She'll get a reputation if she's not careful."

"Miss Knight was already lodging here when I arrived. So maybe it'll be I who gains a reputation." His mother threw him a quelling glance and he raised his brow. "You don't agree, Mother?"

"I care not what Miss Knight does in her own time, so long as it does not impinge or bring scandal to the Duke of Whitstone's doors."

"Like it almost did five years ago? You do realize, do you not, Mother, that I was the one who proposed to Ava and begged her to run away with me to Gretna? It was not the other way around, no matter what you may think."

Lady Clapham's mouth gaped open, and Tate took a calming breath, knowing that what he'd just declared would be all over London before the month was out, thanks to Lady Clapham. Not that he cared. All of the gossiping vipers could go hang.

"If you aspire for me to marry a woman of rank, such as her ladyship present, you are sadly deluded. The woman I marry will be of my choosing. Apologies, Lady Clapham for the bluntness of my tongue, but my mother has an uncanny ability to ignore people's wishes and decrees."

The dowager placed the teacup down with a clatter, spilling a little of the contents over the side on to the saucer. "Ava Knight will never be the Duchess of Whitstone. I forbid it."

"Why are you so against her?" he asked, truly baffled. "Mr. Knight was a gentleman and therefore his daughter is a lady. There is little to dislike from your perspective, I would think."

His Mother rolled her eyes, not something he'd ever thought to see a duchess do before. She stood, rounding on him. "They're common. Her great-grandfather lived in one of the ducal tenant farms before he started horse breeding as a hobby. Please think about that. If you were to have children with this woman, your future son and heir would have a great-grandfather who was a servant in your own home."

Tate had heard enough. He ran a hand through his hair before walking to the door. "How fortunate for father that he did not care for such rules, considering your own heritage, Mother. Common Americans who had money. That was your only claim to some sort of greatness, was it not? In my eyes you're no different to Miss Knight in that sense, except with Ava, she has a heart beating within her chest. I highly doubt you have one at all."

His mother gasped, and Lady Clapham paled. In time Tate might regret the harshness of his words, but today was not that day. "I shall come and see you the day after we arrive back at Berkshire to ensure you've settled in at the dower house. Good afternoon, Mother. Lady Clapham."

CHAPTER 15

*F*ather is unwell, but has insisted I stay in France. He
says it's just a trifling cold, but there was something in
his written words that sent a shiver down my spine. I feel like he's
hiding something from me. Dread has curled in my stomach today and
I cannot shake it.

– An Excerpt from a letter from Miss Ava Knight to the Duke of
Whitstone

*T*wo days after arriving home from London, Ava
stood at the stable doors with her stable
manager, Greg, as Titan's groom walked the stallion
around the mare they wanted him to cover. Today was the
day they would see if Titan liked what he smelled when it
came to Black Lace.

She hoped it was so. Over the last fortnight when
they'd been stabled across from each other the two horses
had seemed to get along reasonably well, and had neighed

once or twice over the stable door, or so the stable boy had informed her, all good signs for a promising union.

"Very good of the duke to give you the approval for the breeding of Titan with Black Lace, Miss Ava. Even if they do not produce a champion, they'll certainly produce pretty foals."

Ava chuckled, supposing that would be true. "And yet that isn't quite what we're hoping to achieve. I'd prefer a champion to a pretty horse." Which wasn't entirely true. Horses, no matter their age or ability would always have her heart. To her, they were truly the best animal on earth.

"The duke mentioned yesterday that there was a break in at old Mr. Rogers' farm, although nothing was stolen, there was evidence that someone tried to light a fire, but it never took. The Runner seems to think it's connected to the fire-starter, but the local magistrate does not. Hard to know what is going on in these parts with all the trouble we've had."

Ava frowned, having not known that another neighbor of hers had been targeted. In fact, she'd not seen Tate at all yesterday. Why did he not call on her? She'd not seen him since they had stayed at the same inn on their way home from London.

Terribly crass of her, but the day she'd excused herself from the dowager in the parlor, she'd dallied in the hall, listening to the duchess' words. Scathing words really, derogatory in fact, and all about her and her unsuitableness as a duchess.

The loathing she'd heard in her voice gave her little hope for friendship. The woman hated her common blood, and as Ava could do nothing about such things, there was little chance of a reconciliation.

She had thought on the prospect of them during the

carriage ride home, watching Tate who rode alongside the vehicle all the way back to her estate. Each time she looked at him her heart squeezed and there was little point denying what that reaction meant.

It was the same that she'd known it when a young girl. She loved him. In all truthfulness, she'd never stopped loving him, no matter how angry she'd been.

But that did not mean they were suitable. That the role of duchess was more important to the role she had here at Knight Stables.

"The duke was here?" she asked, keeping her eye on the horses and feigning an uninterested air that was only skin deep.

"Oh yes, Miss Knight. Came over before luncheon but couldn't stay as he was having luncheon with her grace and Lady Clapham over at the dower house."

"Of course." Ava was quiet as Titan mounted Black Lace. The joining was short, with little fuss, but hopefully successful. "Very good, thank you gentlemen, for your assistance. Now we wait," she said to the yard hands that stood around watching.

"I had thought the duke said he would be here for this, but alas he's been held up, I guess." Greg said, watching the horses.

Ava nodded having thought the same. After all the fuss he'd made about her not having Titan breed with one of her horses, she thought he would not have missed this.

"You may have Titan returned to the ducal farm this afternoon. Their stables are now rebuilt and I know the duke would wish him stabled there. No need in keeping him here any longer." Ava walked over to the stallion and ran her hand down his neck. "Even though he is such a handsome beast." She cooed to the horse for a moment before letting the groom take him back to his stall to prepare him for his walk back to Tate's estate.

"Right you are, Miss Knight. We'll do that directly."

Ava stayed outdoors for the remainder of the afternoon, watching some of the fillies learn how to lunge in the lunging yard, viewing her two hopefuls for the Ascot races do time trails on the gallops before looking over the books for the feed and grain.

She thought on Tate's absence. They had been home two days now, and not a word from him. Was something amiss? Had his mother's wicked tongue finally soured him against her? Ava leaned back in her chair, twisting the quill in her hand as she glanced out the window. Perhaps this was for the best. Their lives were so very different now, both of them had people relying on them, his as a duke and she as a horse breeder and trainer. Their social spheres could not be much further apart, even if one of her friends was a viscountess' niece.

Being home these two days had solidified her dislike of town. She'd missed the stables, of being around her horses, feeding them, simply watching them run about the yards or graze in the meadows. London life was not her forte and being a duchess, a woman of immaculate fashion sense and impeccable friends would not suit her. Why, all her friends from school were as common as she was, besides Willow of course.

Ava sighed and throwing down her quill, stood and started back toward the house. Dinner would be served soon and she'd promised Hallie that she would attend this evening since last night she'd been held up in the lower holding yard after one of her mares had gone through a fence.

Walking up the front drive, she moved out of the way

as the rider who delivered mail cantered from the house, tipping his cap a little as he rode past. Entering the front hall her servant came out of her office, the silver salver in his hand. "Were you looking for me, William?" she asked.

He bowed. "Yes, Miss Knight. A missive from the dowager duchess of Whitstone just arrived. I've placed it on your desk."

"Thank you," she said, going into her office and closing the door. She'd always loved this room, even when it was her father's space and sanctuary. Now it was hers she'd decided not to change a thing about it. The dark mahogany desk, along with bookshelves that lined the walls and two leatherback chairs sat before the hearth ready for anyone to pick up a book, sit and read to their heart's content.

She broke the duchess' seal and scanned the note. The more she read of the missive the more she could not believe the impudence of the woman. How dare she, but then how dare she not? Ava scrunched up the note in her hand and then re-opening it, scanned it for a second time, not believing what she was reading.

*M*iss *Knight,*

I'm having a small ball at my dower house in coming weeks. I know we've had our disagreements in the past, and I do hope for the sake of our small county that we may become more agreeable to one another's presence in time. But unfortunately that time is not now. I am therefore sending this missive as a courtesy, as a small explanation as to why you have not received an invitation. Please do not attend, even at the behest of my son. The dower home is my own and you will not be allowed entrance.

Warmest regards,

Duchess of Whitstone

$\mathcal{F}$or a second time, she screwed up the missive the blood in her veins thumping loud in her ears. How dare the woman? A light knock sounded at the door and Hallie popped her head around the threshold. "Ah, I see you received one as well. I'm so glad that you have. Maybe the dowager has seen that the duke is in love with you and has finally come around to embrace you as a future daughter-in-law."

Ava slumped onto her chair wishing that were so. "No, nothing of the kind, I'm afraid. This is a missive from her grace, but it's a letter telling me not to attend, that I won't be allowed admittance."

"What!" Hallie came into the room, leaving the door ajar. She came over to the desk and snatched the missive from between Ava's fingers, reading it quickly.

"Oh, my, I knew the dowager was cold and cutting, but this is beyond offensive." Hallie met Ava's gaze. "I'm so sorry, Ava. She seems determined to drive a wedge between you and the duke."

That was an underestimation. "Yes, so it would seem."

"What are you going to do? Are you going to tell the duke about this?" she said, waving the note.

Ava shook her head, sick of it all, tired of the constant barbs and bitter looks. The cuts direct in town and nasty notes delivered in the middle of the day. "No. He doesn't need to know about this, it would only make things more awkward."

"But the duke loves you, I'm sure. He's sent his mother to the dower house after all and she was living at Clere-more before."

That was true at least, but it did not change the fact that his mother hated her. A little voice whispered that perhaps their time had come and gone. That they should part now before any further damage to their hearts and families was done.

"Did you receive an invitation?" Ava enquired.

Hallie waved the piece of parchment that was in her other hand. "I did, but I will not attend if you're not going. The dowager inviting me and not you is unreservedly rude and I shall not give her the pleasure of such a slight. We shall stay here together and forget about her grace and her schemes."

Her friend's eyes sparkled with fire and Ava loved her for her loyalty. "You must attend, for if you do not she'll think I had a hand in it. Restricting my friend's outings. Go, enjoy yourself and mingle. Show the dowager duchess of Whitstone that we do not care who she does and does not invite."

"I cannot go without you. I do not care what the dowager will think. I shall stay at home and keep you company."

Ava smiled reaching for her friend's hand. "You will attend, and you will enjoy yourself and tell me all about it when you return. I'm quite content to stay home and I promise you, what her grace does, does not affect me in the lightest. She's interfered and been rude to me for as long as I have known her. She no longer has power over him and she loathes the thought."

Hallie sighed, seemingly unconvinced. "If you're sure, but I do not feel easy over this."

"All will be well, Hallie. Do not concern yourself with me. I'll be quite well at home."

A knock at the door sounded and her butler walked in, announcing the Duke of Whitstone.

Ava stood, her body warming to the sight of him. She schooled her features, meeting Hallie's startled gaze.

"Good afternoon, Your Grace," Hallie said, dipping into a curtsy. "If you'll excuse me, I have some letters to write."

The door closed softly behind her friend and the duke strode over to her, pulling her into his arms and kissing her soundly. She leaned into him, taking all that he would give, relishing his touch, each stroke, touch, kiss that he bestowed on her.

He was impossible to ignore and had always been so.

Tate pulled back, his eyes ablaze with unsated desire. "I've missed you." He pulled her over to the hearth and seated them on the settee. "I've been meaning to call, and I wanted to come here today because we never managed a chance to finish the discussion we started in London."

Dread spiked through her and she sat up straight, folding her hands in her lap. "Our conversation," she queried, stalling.

He nodded. "About us."

"Oh," she said, light-heartedly. "What about us?" The hope that flashed in his stormy gray eyes vanquished her hope that it was about anything but them. She wasn't ready for this conversation or what his reaction would be to her words.

He reached for her hand her own swallowed up by his strong capable ones. "You must know that from the moment I found out that you had not jilted me that all the hurt, the anger I carried with me vanished. I tried to move on from you, even as angry as I was, it did not work and I no longer wish to live without you."

Ava could not tear her attention from him. His words were a balm to her soul, and she wished she could give him all that he wanted, but she could not. Not because she did not love him, burn for him every moment of every day, but because of so many things that stood between them.

She squeezed his hand, adjusting her seat. "You don't have to live without me, Tate, but please don't ask me to be your wife." He flinched at her words and clasped his hand tighter. "Listen to me, please, before you say anything."

He watched her a moment, his eyes guarded. He nodded.

Ava took a fortifying breath, licking her lips. "We were so young when we first fell in love. And it was love, of that I have little doubt. But, having lived abroad for four years, then coming home to run an estate with very little support other than from my staff, I've grown quite independent. I'm financially secure and do not need to marry if I do not wish to." She kept her attention on him, hating the fact that he'd gone an awful shade of gray. "And I do not. To marry would mean the loss of my independence, to not do what I love, whenever I wish. I cannot become an ornament, a woman who talks nonsense and accomplishes little. It's not who I am and having grown up, I know that now."

Tate stood, wrenching his hands free. "I want you to be my wife, Ava, my duchess. What are you asking to be?" His voice was hard, immovable and she cringed.

"I would be your wife tomorrow, Tate, please know that, but I will not be your duchess. It is too much, I would be giving up everything."

"You would not have to give up your life." He ran a frustrated hand through his hair, walking to stand before the fire. He leaned upon the marble mantel, his back to her. "Of course being a duchess comes with responsibilities. Situations that would take you away from here for several months of the year. Is that too much to ask? Are you not willing to give an inch to have me?"

Ava stood, hating the desolated look in his eyes. "I want you, I do. I do not want anyone else. We can still have each other, but not as husband and wife. I will be your lover for as long as you'd want me."

He wrenched from her, disgust twisting his otherwise handsome visage. "I must marry. The family name alone requires me to try for an heir and I will not break my vows to the woman I marry. I will not do that to her, no matter how tempting you are."

Ava bit her lip, panic coursing through her blood. He stepped further away and she stilled. "I will not have you as my mistress. I will not have you at all if I cannot have you as my wife."

Tate turned and strode for the door. Ava ran after him, clutching at his arm. "Please Tate, I cannot lose you again. I simply want…"

"You want it all," he cut in, halting her words. "You want me to scratch your itch whenever it arises. You want to keep your independence and be mistress of your domain. You want me to break my marriage vows to keep your bed warm at night."

She paled, her heart twisting. "Your mother was right I'm not suitable to be your bride. My lineage will always be fodder for town gossip. Our children will be food for the vultures of the *ton* to rip apart and look down upon. I will be ridiculed, gossiped about and ignored. At least as mistress of Knight Stables I am treated with respect. If I became your duchess, all of that would change. They would look for you regarding my horses, the training we offer here. They would look to you for advice and guidance. I will become obsolete, what my family built from the ground up will be obsolete." Ava raised her chin, anger straightening her spine. "I will not have it. Not even for you."

He glanced at her, his eyes void of warmth. "You are wrong, Ava and you are blind to what I can give you. As my wife, my name alone will protect all those that I love, even a woman whose lineage may not be as grand as some, but was grand enough for me."

For a long moment Ava stared at the door that Tate had stormed though, breathless at his declaration. He loved her? Never in all the time they'd been together had he uttered the words. She had silently hoped she was not alone in her affections and now she knew she was not. Ava walked to the window, watching as he rode off down her drive as if the devil himself was behind him.

A cold shiver ran down her spine that perhaps she'd been wrong, had made a mistake, one that this time she would not be able to undo.

CHAPTER 16

a fortnight had passed and Tate had not seen Ava, or more truthfully he'd avoided her after their parting. He stared down at the whisky in his hand, reminding himself that no matter how many he imbibed, it would not make him feel any better, would not numb the hurt that coursed through his veins every minute of every day.

She had rejected him.

He clenched his jaw, looking up toward the door as the butler announced more of his mother's guests at her ball, another useless, non-essential evening. He glanced about the room. The people laughed, drank, took more wine and food from the waiting servants. Useless beings all of them. Spoiled and entitled.

Was it no wonder Ava did not want to be part of this life. He did not either.

Tate stood beside Lord Duncannon, his friend as quiet as he, and thankfully not trying to fill the silence between them. He did not wish to speak as it was, not to anyone here at least.

A rumble of chatter sounded and Tate again glanced toward the door. Hope surged through him as he recognized Miss Evans. His eyes moved past her, searching for another set of dark russet eyes and hair to match and found her missing. He pushed away his disappointment, drinking down the amber liquid and watched as Miss Evans bustled her way over to him, literally repositioning people who stood in her way.

Miss Evans came to stand before him and he spoke before she got a word in. "Where is Ava?" he demanded. The two women were very rarely apart at such gatherings, and so Ava should be here.

"Dear God, I did not think I'd ever see you again." Lord Duncannon gaped at Ava's friend, his face paling.

"Hoped would be a better word I think, Lord Duncannon," Miss Evans retorted, her eyes blazing with fire, but not before a flush stole over her cheeks leaving them a pretty shade of pink. "Or at least it was, in my case." She turned her penetrating gaze toward Tate and he looked between the pair wondering how on earth they knew each other.

He dismissed the thought a moment, needing to know where Ava was. "Is Miss Knight here this evening, Miss Evans?"

"She did not receive an invitation, but I convinced her to come, Your Grace." His attention shifted to his Mother at this declaration and anger spiked through him. This time she'd gone too far.

Miss Evans pursed her lips, inspected him like one inspected a bug and found it wanting. "I'm going to speak plainly and forgive me if I overstep my bounds, but Ava is my friend and I need to say what I must."

Tate nodded, steeling himself for what was undoubtably a set-down to come.

"Your mother sent Ava a note telling her why she would not be invited tonight and Ava is in no doubt as to what your mother thinks of her. Just now, in fact, she was refused entry, in front of all these people you claim to be your friends. What say you, Your Grace? What will your course be?"

"Where is Ava now?" Lord Duncannon demanded.

"She's returned home in the carriage." Miss Evans kept her attention on Tate even though she had answered his friend's question.

The public slight to Ava was unacceptable. Tate would not allow his mother anywhere near him or the ducal property again after this atrocious behavior. He shouldn't even be here for that matter. And he should've acted earlier on his emotions that drove him regarding Ava. He should have returned to her home, on bended knees, begging forgiveness, asking her to love him as much as he loved her. Tell her that he'd never wished to box her in, demand of her more than she was willing to give. Tell her that he loved her more than any title.

"Fuck," he cursed, not heeding those about him.

He started toward the ballroom door, leaving Duncannon and Miss Evans to follow close on his heels.

Duncannon caught up to him. "Where are you going?"

"To get my duchess," he said aloud, not caring who heard him. Gasps sounded about him, and he schooled his temper as his mother stepped in front of him, stalling his escape.

"Move out of the way, mother."

The room stilled, dancers halted and conversation stopped. Even the orchestra ceased to play. "There is about to be a waltz, Tate dear. Would you dance with Lady Clapham?" His mother gestured toward her ladyship who curtsied and smiled knowingly at him, her eyes twinkling with mirth.

"Your Grace, I would be honored," Lady Clapham said, ignoring the fact he was leaving.

"I will not," he said, causing more gasps and barely audible whispers.

His mother laughed a nervous edge to it. Good, he hoped she was uneasy. He'd certainly given up all hope of his last remaining parent supporting the woman he loved and wanted to marry. His mother would pay for being blinded by her hate and exclusivity.

"The ball has only just begun and as Lady Clapham is my guest of honor, you must dance with her. It's only right."

"You disinvited and refused entry to Miss Knight. Are you so full of hate that you cannot remember that you too were common born, rich yes, but the same as Ava. The duchess' coronet is all that separates you from her. You should not have airs when none are justified."

His mother narrowed her eyes, raising her chin. "She is not for you, Son. Do not make the mistake that would bring our family scandal and to its knees. She's a lowly horse farmer. Please, be sensible."

"Ava is more than that and you damn well know it." He stepped past her, Duncannon and Miss Evans following close behind. Striding through the front hall, he didn't wait for a footman and opened the door himself, calling for a carriage.

"Are you going to Miss Knight's estate?" Duncannon asked as a carriage came about the house.

Tate stilled as an acrid stench wafted across his senses.

"Can you smell that?" He walked further onto the drive, looking out over the land now kissed by night.

"There is a fire somewhere." Miss Evans came up beside him as the carriage pulled up before the front doors. "It's nearby, or we wouldn't smell it."

"Come," he said to both of them, heading toward the carriage and giving directions to Miss Knight's home.

The closer they came to Ava's estate, the heavier the smell of burning wood permeated the air and as they came over the small rise where Ava's home came into view, the horrifying sight of her stables along with her home in full flame was revealed.

Through the haze of smoke, he could hear yelling and the sounds of horses' hooves as they were released from the stables. Some frightened horses bolted past them and Tate yelled out to the driver to go.

"I should never have let her leave the ball. I should have made her come with me."

"This is not your fault, Miss Evans," Duncannon said, his voice surprisingly soothing in a situation that was anything but calm.

Tate's throat closed in panic and he fought to breathe. Where is she? Madness was all about them and until he saw her with his own eyes, held her close, he would not rest.

The closer they came to the fire the thicker the smoke, and by the time they pulled up a little distance away from the main house, Tate could see one whole side of the home was alight.

Servants ran in and out of the house, grabbing as much of Ava's ancestral belongings as they could. Tate bolted from the carriage. He scanned each and every one of them and not seeing Ava he looked up at the house, praying she wasn't inside.

He threw off his evening jacket and clasped the butler by his arm as he was about to dash back inside. "Where is Ava?" he shouted over the noise of the fire and those yelling orders about them.

"We cannot find her, Your Grace. She returned from the duchess' ball an hour ago, at the time that the fire commenced. She went to her room, but when we checked there we could not find her."

Tate searched the faces running about praying one of them was Ava. Miss Evans and Duncannon caught up to him, their breathing as ragged as his own.

"What can we do, Tate?" his friend asked.

Tate fought not to panic. He looked about again, praying, hoping that he would spy her. He looked back up at the house, half of which was well alight. Was she inside? If she were, he'd not rest until she was safe. She'd risked her life to help him escape his stable fire and he would not leave her alone in this.

"Search the grounds, the stables, maybe Ava is there. Come back here if you cannot find her. I'll check the house."

Duncannon clutched his arm, hard. "You cannot go in there, Tate. You're the last of the Whitstone line. If you die, the title reverts to the crown. Let us search the stable first, you have a look about the perimeter of the house, maybe Ava is fighting the fire with the men on the opposite side."

"I will check there first, but if I cannot find her, I will be going inside. Be damned the title." Ava meant more to him than what he had inherited. His title did not define who he was, it was his character which did that, and he would not be a man who left a woman, his woman to burn to death.

Lord Duncannon nodded, seemingly resigning himself to Tate's decree. "Very well." He paused for a moment. "Miss Evans, come, we'll check the stables."

She left without a word and taking another look at those about him and still not seeing Ava, Tate ran around the side of the house. Still, Ava was nowhere to be seen, and panic started to rise up in his blood.

Please be safe, my darling. Don't be in the house.

The doors to the kitchens were open, and Tate ran for them, moving out of the way as servant after servant came out carrying whatever they could save.

Tate ran past them all, up a smoke-filled corridor to stumble into the front hall of the home. Doors to the burning wing were closed, but smoke filled the space. He coughed, untying his cravat and tying it about his mouth and nose to help him breathe.

Taking the stairs two at a time, he called out for Ava, and yet only the crackling, the moaning of a house that would be ash by morning sounded in the night.

~

*A*va stood inside the door to her room, watching as Lord Oakes paced her bedchamber floor, seemingly oblivious to the raging fire that was devastating her home.

Her *home*, the place she had been born, the house her parents had built through years of hard work was crumbling about her and there was little she or anyone could do. She blinked as the smoke thickened, clogged her lungs and stung her eyes. Her eyes flicked to the window, her only escape, but she was a floor up and a fall from this height would break her neck. She edged toward it, willing to take the risk.

"Don't even think about it." Lord Oakes stepped in front of her, his features contorted into raw hate.

"Why are you doing this?" He leaned toward her leaving little space between them. "What are you getting out of such deeds?" she asked, coughing with the effort to speak.

"I left the best for last," he seethed. "You were supposed to be my mistress, the woman who warmed my bed, and yet you spread your legs for that bastard Whitstone."

She gaped at him. The man was mad! "You were jealous! That's why you started the fires about our county." Ava could not believe what he was saying. Surely he was not so obsessed with her that he would act out in such a way. Her neighbors were innocent people, they did not deserve this.

"None of them were innocent," he said, gesturing toward the outdoors. "Whitstone had your heart, always has had, and those blasted Mortons, his wife supported and comforted you over Whitstone. I could not allow such deeds to go unpunished."

Ava shook her head. "I will never warm your bed, Lord Oakes. You have proven yourself to be the worst of men, not just this night, but from the day you tried to force yourself upon me in this very house." She tried to think of Tate, of how he warmed her blood, comforted and protected her. Not to freeze in panic over the thought of what Lord Oakes was doing with her in this room. What his ultimate goal was for this night.

He stabbed a finger at her chest. Ava raised her chin,

refusing to wince at the pain it caused. "Before this night, I shall sample your flesh, and I will enjoy every second of it. My desire to have you blinded me and it was because of you that my betrothed broke our understanding. She sensed I was not committed, so you see," he said, running a hand over her bodice. "I lost the bride that would fill my coffers all because of you. But alas, I have a plan."

Ava schooled her features as panic licked at her skin, willing her to flee, to run, even into the flames on the other side of the door simply to get away from him. She swallowed her throat dry and sore from the smoke, and tears pricked her eyes.

The image of Tate flittered through her mind that she would not see him again if Lord Oakes had his way and a cavernous chasm opened in her chest. She'd been a selfish fool. A silly, little idiot who could not see the wonderful gift that Tate offered when he laid it at her feet.

His love.

And she loved him, everything else would fit in and around that love and they would make their difficult, busy lives merge. If she made it out of here alive, that was.

"Your obsession has killed people, you should hang for your crimes."

He shrugged. "The lad was a lowly servant. They're expendable and I care not at all what happens to anyone that gets in my way, or your precious horses."

Rage tore through her at the mention of her horses and Ava set upon him. They fell to the ground and she scratched at his face, anything to hurt him. "You better not have touched my horses," she yelled, hating him with every fiber of her being.

He wrestled to clutch her arms and she punched him, trying to hurt him as much as she could so to escape. Lord

Oakes reached up and clasped her hair, pulling it hard. Ava came down on her side, pain ricocheting through her head as he pinned her to the floor.

"Bitch," he seethed at her ear, his spirit-heavy breath turning her stomach. "Shall I have you now, Miss Knight? We're both going to die, a good fuck before we do is just what I need."

Fear held her immobile for a moment, before fight took hold and she lifted her leg as much as she could, trying to hit him between the legs where men are especially sensitive to pain.

He sensed her thoughts and pinned her legs with his own. "You're going to hang for this, you bastard."

He chuckled. "I have nothing left, so what does it matter if they stretch my neck, but my darling, Ava." He leaned down, kissing her hard. His teeth knocked her lips and her mouth filled with a metallic taste. Ava leaned into the kiss and bit his bottom lip, hard.

He squealed and wrenched back, but she refused to let go before his hands came about her neck, squeezing the breath from her lungs.

Lord Oakes stood, clasping his mouth. Ava fought for breath, watching him from the floor as her mind raced to save herself. A loud crash sounded somewhere in the house and the smoke thickened, the room choking them both of life.

He walked around her and she sat up, wiping her mouth of both their blood. "I will fight you until my last breath, you bastard. I will not be your victim."

Lord Oakes rushed her, kicking her hard against her hip. She gasped at the pain of his attack but instead of rolling away, she clasped his legs, pinning them together and halting him from doing it again.

Then she bit him, again.

He swore and a sense of power ran through her blood. Damn bastard burned her home and stables down would he? Hurt her horses. Well, he too would hurt this night. She would not be the only one to come out of this bloody and bruised, if she came out of this at all.

He fell over and Ava took the opportunity to get up and run for the window. She glanced at the door, a red glow flicking beneath the wood. Smoke slithered along the cornice of the wall like a snake and there would be little time left to leave. She had to get out now or she'd die.

Ava reached to unlock the window, hoisting up the pane. She screamed as he caught her about the stomach, wrenching her back. Instead of landing on the floor, this time she hit the bed and Lord Oakes came down over her, his eyes wild with hate and determination.

Blood dripped on her face from his bloody lip and she pushed at him, scratched at him to no avail. He was too heavy, too resolute.

Her throat closed in panic at the similarities to when he tried to rape her all those months ago. She fought not to panic, to freeze in fear. "Get off, you bastard," she screamed.

He wrenched her gown up and air kissed her thighs. His movements were harried and desperate as he tugged at his front falls.

No. No. No! This could not happen to her, this could not be happening. Her body shook and she brought her knees up, trying to wedge them between him and herself, denying him what he wanted.

The roof gave an awful moan, and dropped, exposing the flames beyond. She was going to die. She was going to die as he raped her.

No.

"You think I don't have time. I cannot think of a better way to die than deep inside your cunny."

"Noooo," she screamed, wrestling him, the thought of such a horror pulling forth the last of her strength. He would not win. He could not win. Life could not be so unfair.

Shock registered on Lord Oakes' face, and a yelp expelled from his mouth before he was dragged from her body and she was free.

Ava shuffled off the bed as Tate slammed his fist into Lord Oakes' face, the crunch of bone and teeth smashing rent the air. An endless drubbing of blows rained down on his lordship, Tate's visage one of deadly ire. She shivered, having never seen him so mad. He would kill him if he continued. Not that she cared about Lord Oakes, but she did not want his death to be a burden on Tate's conscience for the rest of his life. She went up to Tate, clutching his arm as he went to hit Lord Oakes yet again. "Stop before you kill him. Let the authorities mete out the punishment, not you."

His muscles beneath her palm were taut and his breathing ragged. The fire took hold of the curtains and she pulled him toward the window. "We need to go. This room will be full alight any moment."

Lord Oakes mumbled something and then sat up, stumbling toward the door. "I should've shot you both that day in the field. It is the one regret I shall live with for the rest of my life."

Ava looked out the window ignoring the mad man's words. A downpipe ran along the corner of the house. It might hold their weight… "Come, we need to climb down."

Tate stood between Ava and Lord Oakes and didn't move. "You're going to hang for this," he yelled. "That will be something that I will ensure happens to you."

Lord Oakes smirked, wrenching the door open. He stepped out into the burning corridor before running into the flames beyond. Ava stared as his clothes caught alight, his hair aflame, before he disappeared into the smoke and burning house.

"He's dying," she said, not believing what just occurred.

"Let him." Tate strode over to her and wrapped his arm about her waist, helping her to climb out the window. The pipe thankfully held both their weight and Ava climbed down, some of her staff waiting at the bottom, should she fall.

Tate followed her, jumping from the pipe at the last minute just as an almighty crash sounded. Ava stood back from the house as the roof caved in, destroying all that lay beneath it. She swiped at the tears that ran down her cheeks. The house now fully engulfed in flames, there was little anyone could do.

Tate came over to her and held her close. Uncontrollable shivers raked her body and she bundled against him, seeking his warmth and comfort. Tate called for a blanket, and a maid ran to them, giving him one. He wrapped it about her, stroking her back. "I'm sorry I didn't get to you quicker. Are you hurt?"

Her soul was hurt, and she was shaken, but thankfully Tate had arrived in time. "I'll be all right. I'm sad, that is all." She blinked trying to stem her tears, but to no avail. "My home…"

"I know," he said, holding her tighter. "We'll rebuild it."

She looked up at him, wiping her nose with the back of her hand. Not the most ladylike action, but right at this moment she did not care. "I know, but it'll not be the same."

"We'll make it the same, darling." He didn't let her go and nor did she want him to. Not now or ever. With Tate she was safe, loved and respected, he was an honorable man, a good man and her heart swelled with love for him.

"Your Grace," a voice rang out and Tate and Ava turned to see one of the undercover Bow Street runners striding their way.

The growl from Tate sounded beside her. "How did this happen? You were supposed to be watching Lord Oakes' every move," Tate said, pointing a finger at the man.

The Runner sighed, running a hand through his already rumpled hair. "When Miss Knight left for the ball, we can only surmise that Lord Oakes used the opportunity to steal into her home. Lay in wait until she returned." The Runner turned to Ava, placing his hand over his heart. "We're truly sorry, Miss Knight. Tonight we have failed you."

"We shall discuss this further in a few days' time at my estate, and I suggest you find out where the lapse in observation has occurred. I want to know." Tate pulled her harder against him, his warmth and care serving as a balm. Her eyes drooped as a sudden rush of tiredness swamped her.

The Runner bowed, stepping back. "Of course, Your Grace."

Ava glanced up at Tate, clutching the lapels of his evening wear. "You saved me," she said, her voice wobbling at the admission.

His gaze shot to her, surprise written on his handsome face. "Always." A pained expression crossed his features. "You are everything to me. When I saw what Lord Oakes was attempting, what he may have already done. If the fire had not killed him, I would have. I promise you he will never hurt you again or anyone else for that matter."

"I'm so sorry, Tate," she admitted. Her heart hurt at how foolish she'd been. The time she'd lost by holding on to a life that only ever half fulfilled her. No matter what she'd told herself, there had always been a piece of her missing. Until that piece had stepped back into her life.

Tate.

"I was holding onto my past and couldn't see straight," she continued. "I let what others thought of me, blind me to what I wanted. I let prejudice against me make me believe I was not worthy of you. But not any longer. I can see clearly now. I want a future with you. I want our lives to merge in every way. I want to make us work and let everything else fall about us as it will."

He smiled, pulling her closer. "You're not the only one who has been blinded by their own dreams. Of course, I want you by my side, my wife, my duchess, but I do not expect you to be away from here for months on end and it was selfish of me to think you could be. London is not so very far away, and when Parliament sits, or the Season calls me to town, I do not expect you to leave your responsibilities for such frivolities. Here is what matters the most." He ran his hands over her hair, linking them at her nape. "What I said the last time we spoke I meant. I love you, so very much. I cannot live without you."

Her eyes smarted as his voice cracked at his last words and she stepped up to wrap her arms about his neck, holding him close. "I love you too," she whispered against his ear. He turned his head to look at her and she smiled. Ava closed the space between them and kissed him, heedless of those about them. Tate didn't shy away and ravenously took her mouth, making her forget all the troubles of the night and warming the chill from her blood.

A discreet cough pulled them from each other and they looked to see Hallie and Lord Duncannon standing at their sides, amusement written across their faces. Soot and dirt stained their ballroom clothing, their faces and hands.

Hallie stepped toward them, enclosing them both in a hug. "I'm so relieved you're safe," Hallie said, her eyes overly bright. "We got caught up trying to save the horses. With you not at the stables, we stayed and offered assistance and thankfully no horses have been lost."

"We will have to round them up though in the morning. Most have bolted from the grounds," Lord Duncannon stated.

All of which was understandable from the trauma the animals suffered, all because Lord Oakes had been a madman. A man so blinded with jealousy at not getting what he wanted and so he had acted out, punished those whom he assumed to be at fault in hindering his ends. Ava shook her head. How could anyone be so evil?

"Come, there is little we can do here. We'll travel back to Cleremore and you both will stay with me for the duration of the rebuild of your home and stables."

Ava nodded. There was little she could do here, everything was gone. They would return in the morning and look for the horses, which hopefully had not run too far away. They made their way over to the ducal carriage, and Ava gave her thanks when Tate helped her inside, her legs threatening to give way beneath her.

She glanced out the carriage window and looked at

what was left of her home, and despair swamped her. How could Lord Oakes do such a thing? A question she would probably ask herself for many years to come.

"Are you ready?" the duke asked, coming to sit beside her and taking her in his arms, pulling her close to his side.

Ava nodded, not wanting to see any more of the destruction of her home before she was prepared to face it. "I am more than ready."

ather has died and I'm on my way home. I have lost everything it seems, you, my father, but at least I have my horses. I suppose that is some comfort in a time when I have none.

– An Excerpt from a letter from Miss Ava Knight to the Duke of Whitstone

A month later, Tate stood outside Ava's ruined home, and watched as the first lumber arrived for the new structure to be built. Last week carts arrived filled with stone, and now the builders were salvaging whatever they could of the old house's building material to use again.

The estate was a flurry of work, and Tate glanced across the yard and watched as Ava discussed things with the man they'd hired to rebuild the home and stables.

A smile lifted his lips. She was so beautiful, capable, and his heart ached at the sight of her. She caught sight of him staring and she gave him a knowing smile. Somehow she'd always know what he was thinking, feeling. Ava Knight was truly his perfect match.

He turned back to the house, shaking his head at the destruction. Lord Oakes had ensured nothing would survive and it had not. Except for the few pieces of furniture and valuables the staff had been able to carry outside before the fire took hold too much.

The local magistrate had declared his death an accident, and knowing that the man had admitted his crimes to Ava before his demise, the authorities were willing to let the case close and be done with it.

Tate was happy for this outcome. After what he'd seen Lord Oakes trying to do to Ava the night of the fire, he would've gutted him on the lawn had he escaped, the bastard deserved nothing less.

Ava sidled up to him, clasping his arm and holding him close. "It's going to be like the fire never happened when we're finished with it. Don't you agree?" she asked, looking up at him.

He tweaked her sweet nose. "With one little difference," he said, smiling, indulging himself with a kiss from her charming lips.

She glanced at his expectantly. "And what would that be?" she asked.

Tate chuckled. "After tomorrow, you'll return here a duchess and my wife." At the words, contentment settled over him, soothing his soul.

Her hand shifted from his arm to wrap about his waist. "Yes, and you will return as my husband."

He wrapped his arms about her and kissed her heedless of the workers about them. And even when whistles and laugher penetrated his brain he did not stop. Would never stop loving the woman in his arms, no matter where or who they were about.

They would be the Duke and Duchess of Whitstone and they made their own rules, made their own decisions and that would never change.

EPILOGUE

Two years and four months later.

*A*va shouted out from the ducal box at Ascot as Titan flew down the straight, the other horses hard on his heels and yet the stallion showed no signs of slowing down. She stood, yelling out across the swarm of heads before her in the stands, Tate by her side, laughing and yelling with her as their horse crossed the line the winner.

For a moment they stared at each other in amazement, before Ava jumped into his arms, tears smarting and her heart beating loud in her chest. They'd won! They'd won Ascot!

"I don't believe it," Lord Duncannon said beside them. "I've won a fortune."

Ava laughed, not believing it herself. "You must go down, Tate. Collect the cup and ribbon."

He glanced at her, clearly still shocked at what had occurred. Ava glanced back at the racetrack and smiled as the jockey riding Titan trotted him back toward where they would receive the prize.

Tate kissed her cheek quickly before running down the stairs, heading toward their horse. Many people about them congratulated them and Ava thanked them in turn, wanting to remember every moment of this day for the rest of her life.

During the first two years of their marriage they had worked hard to get both stables back up and running, and thankfully the horses had not suffered too much from the trauma Lord Oakes had caused.

"If only Hallie was here to see this. She would love this so much," she said aloud. Lord Duncannon's smile slipped a little at the mention of her friend and Ava couldn't help but wonder what had happened between the pair. "She would be happy for you. I have no doubt."

Ava glanced to where Tate stood his smile wide, making him look like the most handsome man in the world. He shook the jockey's hand before giving Titan a big pat on his neck.

"Have you heard from her?" Lord Duncannon asked.

Ava's attention snapped back to him, having not expected him to be so forward. "She arrives back in London next week if the ship from Egypt is not delayed."

His lordship did look at her then and Ava didn't miss the unhidden interest in his eyes. She grinned at him, wagging one finger. "One of these days you're going to tell me why you both look sheepish when around each other. Tate and I know you are both not telling us something."

He chuckled and she shook her head. Even Tate did not know what had passed between the pair, but by God, Ava would dearly love to know. When they traveled to London next week to collect Hallie she would demand to know. Not that Hallie would probably tell her anything. The woman was like a safe that secrets never escaped from.

Ava clapped as Tate took possession of the Gold cup and she smiled down at him as he lifted it toward her. Pride seized her, for them both at their day's success.

"I'm sure you're looking forward to seeing Miss Evans again."

Ava nodded. "Of course," she replied. "There is an artifact they wanted brought back to the British Museum. They surmised that because Hallie had contacts here, that she would be best to travel with the artifact." Ava shook the hands of a trainer who came to congratulate them. "I, for one, cannot wait to see her again. I do hope she stays a little longer this time."

Lord Duncannon nodded, smiling and Ava turned back to follow Tate's progress back to them through the bevy of congratulations and well wishes in the crowd.

"You do realize we'll not hear the end of this win for years to come," she said, laughing when Tate kissed the Gold cup in his hands.

Duncannon chuckled. "I do believe you are right, duchess."

Tate made it back to her and he handed her the cup. Marrying the duke had been the best decision she'd ever made, and even though his mother had never forgiven them and still refused to apologize for her atrocious behavior, the past two years had been the happiest of her life and she couldn't imagine a time any longer when they were not married.

"Congratulations, darling. You should've come down and received the cup with me. This is yours as much as mine."

She looked over the prize, smiling. "I will, next year when one of my horses race and wins."

Tate laughed, kissing her and not caring who saw, an action that he did often. If there was one thing Tate loved to do was scandalize the *ton*. Which, she had to admit, she enjoyed also.

AUTHOR NOTE

As you've probably noticed, I did take some creative license in regards to who actually won the Ascot Gold Cup in 1823. While I'd love to think Titan would've been good enough to win, the actual winner that year was a horse named, Marcellus. Marcellus was a four-year-old thoroughbred ridden by Will Wheatley, trained by William Chifney and owned by the Earl of Darlington.

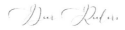

Thank you for taking the time to read *Tempt Me, Your Grace*! I hope you enjoyed the first book in my League of Unweddable Gentlemen series. I've always loved horses, had one growing up, and so I wanted to write a story that had horses at the centre of it.

I'm forever grateful to my readers, so if you're able, I would appreciate an honest review of *Tempt Me, Your Grace*. As they say, feed an author, leave a review!

If you'd like to learn about book two in my League of Unweddable Gentlemen series, *Hellion at Heart*, please read on. I have included chapter one for your reading pleasure.

Tamara Gill

HELLION AT HEART

LEAGUE OF UNWEDDABLE GENTLEMEN,
BOOK 2

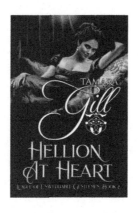

Sifting through the sands in the Middle East while learning of ancient cultures and buried civilizations is all Miss Hallie Evans dreams about. But when an impending scandal forces her back to England, her hopes and dreams are destroyed. Now, as a hired archaeologist for the rich, Hallie explores and studies the ancient ruins excavated on their properties.

. . .

The Viscount of Duncannon, Arthur Howard, was beguiled after a chance encounter with Miss Hallie Evans several years ago. She left an impression on him that never faded. But when their paths cross again, Arthur is determined to win Hallie's heart this time around--at all costs.

But as Hallie's buried secrets begin to surface, neither can stop society from unearthing the truth. Now, Arthur must choose between love and family duty. Can Hallie cease those who threaten her livelihood for a real chance at true love?

CHAPTER 1

Surrey 1813

*H*allie sat at the breakfast table with her papa, reading over the latest articles that had come out of Egypt and the wonderful finds of the ancient land that had been buried for thousands of years.

She sighed, looking out the window at the dreary, wet morning, dreaming of the heat, the sand and culture. Where spices floated in the air and invigorated the soul. Not like her life here in Surrey, where she did little except tend the garden and read in the library.

Her father cleared his throat, gaining her attention. "Hallie dear, there is something that I need to discuss with you. It is of great importance, so please let me finish before you say anything."

Hallie set down her paper, and turned to her papa. "Of course."

Her father, a gentleman, but one with limited land and fortune smiled a little and she frowned, wondering why he appeared so nervous. A light sheen of sweat formed on his forehead, and, picking up his napkin, he dabbed it away.

"My darling girl, this is not easy for me to tell you, and please know that I do this only because I have your best interest at heart."

She sat back in her chair, a hard knot forming in her stomach. "Of course," she managed, although she feared this conversation would be unlike any they had had before. Something was wrong, but what that was she partially didn't wish to know.

"I'm sending you away to a school in France. The Madame Dufour's Refining School for Girls is highly recommended and with your love of history, I think this will be good for you. You're never going to achieve your dreams by only reading the books in my library. All of which are sadly lacking and will be even more so in the months to come."

"You're sending me away? Why, Papa? I do not understand."

He sighed, reaching across the table to take her hand. His touch was warm and yet the idea of leaving Surrey, her papa, left her cold.

"I may have been born a gentleman, the fourth son of a baron, but simply being related to the aristocracy, no matter how distant, does not earn you funds. I have kept the house for as long as I could, but it was of no use and only yesterday I'm happy to say that I have sold it."

Hallie gasped, pulling her hand away. "You sold our home?"

Her father ignored her accusatory tone and nodded. "I did, and with the funds I have purchased myself a small cottage in Felday. It's a two-bedroom cottage that looks out onto the town square and it'll do us nicely I think. All our possessions that we can fit will come with us, the books also, and so I think we can make the cottage our own and be very comfortable there."

She shook her head, not believing what she was hearing. "Papa, our life is here. I was born in this very room. My last memories of Mama are here. Please, reconsider."

Her father pushed back his chair, scraping the feet against the floor. Hallie grimaced as he went to stand at the window, overlooking the hollyhocks and roses outside.

"Do you not think I know this, my dear? Do you not know that it broke my heart to sell our home, but it was either that, walk away with some funds, or walk away with nothing? I chose the former. The sale was profitable, and I have enough to keep me for the rest of my days, and to give you a small dowry along with your schooling in France."

He turned and strode over to her, pulling Hallie to stand. "You must promise me to use your time at school to better yourself. Arm yourself with so much knowledge that nothing and no one can stand in your way. That you will run with your smarts that I know you have and make a life from it. See the world, visit your beloved Egypt you're always reading about," he said, looking down at her article, "and live a full and happy life. Just as I and your mama always hoped for. You are always welcome at the cottage when you're home."

Hallie swallowed the lump in her throat, having never heard her father speak in such a way before. "I promise, Papa. I shall make you proud and before I go, together we'll ensure the cottage is just how we like it. Make it our new home away from this one."

Her papa pulled her into a fierce embrace and Hallie wrapped her arms about him, noticing for the first time how fragile and so much older he was than she realized. She squeezed him harder, wishing life to just halt a moment, to pause and stay as it was.

"I'm glad you said that, my dear. For I have old Farmer McKinnon coming tomorrow with his cart to help us shift. It'll be a busy two days."

Her father walked to the door, heading toward the foyer. Hallie followed him. "Two days. Why two days?" she asked.

He turned, smiling. "Because we have to be out of the house in two days. I suggest you finish breakfast and start packing."

Hallie stared after him, shutting her mouth with a snap. The house was not small, and the idea of packing, picking what they would keep and leave behind left her momentarily stunned. However would they do it with one house maid, a cook and one groomsman who also acted as their butler?

Shaking her head, but never one to shy away from hard work, Hallie called out to Maisie, her maid, for assistance. If they only had two days, then it would only take her two days to complete the relocation of their belongings. She rolled up her sleeves, heading toward the stairs. "I think I'll start with the guest bedroom first and work my way through," she said aloud to herself. Determined to hit her father's deadline and roll with the stones life throws at one's self, dodging accordingly.

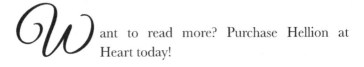

ant to read more? Purchase *Hellion at Heart* today!

ALSO BY TAMARA GILL

Royal House of Atharia Series

TO DREAM OF YOU

A ROYAL PROPOSITION

FOREVER MY PRINCESS

ROYAL ATHARIA - BOOKS 1-3 BUNDLE

League of Unweddable Gentlemen Series

TEMPT ME, YOUR GRACE

HELLION AT HEART

DARE TO BE SCANDALOUS

TO BE WICKED WITH YOU

KISS ME DUKE

THE MARQUESS IS MINE

LEAGUE - BOOKS 1-3 BUNDLE

LEAGUE - BOOKS 4-6 BUNDLE

Kiss the Wallflower series

A MIDSUMMER KISS

A KISS AT MISTLETOE

A KISS IN SPRING

TO FALL FOR A KISS

A DUKE'S WILD KISS

TO KISS A HIGHLAND ROSE

KISS THE WALLFLOWER - BOOKS 1-3 BUNDLE

KISS THE WALLFLOWER - BOOKS 4-6 BUNDLE

Lords of London Series

TO BEDEVIL A DUKE

TO MADDEN A MARQUESS

TO TEMPT AN EARL

TO VEX A VISCOUNT

TO DARE A DUCHESS

TO MARRY A MARCHIONESS

LORDS OF LONDON - BOOKS 1-3 BUNDLE

LORDS OF LONDON - BOOKS 4-6 BUNDLE

To Marry a Rogue Series

ONLY AN EARL WILL DO

ONLY A DUKE WILL DO

ONLY A VISCOUNT WILL DO

ONLY A MARQUESS WILL DO

ONLY A LADY WILL DO

TO MARRY A ROGUE - BOOKS 1-5 BUNDLE

A Time Traveler's Highland Love Series

TO CONQUER A SCOT

TO SAVE A SAVAGE SCOT

TO WIN A HIGHLAND SCOT

HIGHLAND LOVE - BOOKS 1-3 BUNDLE

A Stolen Season Series

A STOLEN SEASON

A STOLEN SEASON: BATH

A STOLEN SEASON: LONDON

Time Travel Romance

DEFIANT SURRENDER

Scandalous London Series

A GENTLEMAN'S PROMISE

A CAPTAIN'S ORDER

A MARRIAGE MADE IN MAYFAIR

SCANDALOUS LONDON - BOOKS 1-3 BUNDLE

High Seas & High Stakes Series

HIS LADY SMUGGLER

HER GENTLEMAN PIRATE

HIGH SEAS & HIGH STAKES - BOOKS 1-2 BUNDLE

Daughters Of The Gods Series

BANISHED-GUARDIAN-FALLEN

DAUGHTERS OF THE GODS - BOOKS 1-3 BUNDLE

Stand Alone Books

TO SIN WITH SCANDAL

OUTLAWS

ABOUT THE AUTHOR

Tamara is an Australian author who grew up in an old mining town in country South Australia, where her love of history was founded. So much so, she made her darling husband travel to the UK for their honeymoon, where she dragged him from one historical monument and castle to another.

A mother of three, her two little gentlemen in the making, a future lady (she hopes) and a part-time job keep her busy in the real world, but whenever she gets a moment's peace she loves to write romance novels in an array of genres, including regency, medieval and time travel.

www.tamaragill.com
tamaragillauthor@gmail.com